I0685296

Baby Loves Magic

Jason Heath Christensen, Ph.D.

Gabriel Maverick Publishing House

2025

Baby Loves Magic

Published by Gabriel Maverick Publishing House

Copyright @ 2025 by Jason Heath Christensen

Cover art: "Excalibur Raging Hell" by Jason Heath Christensen

All rights reserved.

ISBN: 979-8-9881775-1-7

My Ethos

If I could make all the animals happy,

My life would be a job well done.

I'd free them from captivity,

And give them miles to run.

I know my dog is a prince,

Because when I treat him like one,

He is pleased.

I feel so close to this animal,

As if we share the same mind:

Too young to fade away.

I just have to stop off in my life,

To give a dog a good life.

My dog Maverick was just beginning to discover life,

When I thought mine was over.

Simple, just…

A dog's joy,

Running across a field…

Lost in the wind,

A dog's bark,

Time rushing…

Maverick My Boy

Poverty and illiteracy

Are the times to sit quietly in the sun,

Crisis bashing your skull from all sides.

You didn't even have childhood to begin with,

Condemner of all my youth.

And now that youth is lost, torn, Christ-like gone,

Only wilted hope remains –

Too hollow for tears,

Indefensible belief.

Big people are bored,

Preparing for their deaths,

While the well-cared-for dogs are joyous

From dawn till dusk.

Because the forgetful human mind

Loses glee before all things,

While the nurtured dog is free – ten times man's glee!

If you can pluck an apple from a tree

And eat it without fear,

Then you win:

A dog's heart is your honor.

Pet him lovingly –

He knows every aspect of your soul,

Even more than you yourself sometimes care to recall,

As you hide in the adult human shadows

Of mistrust and rejection.

Forgiveness is a virtue

Most natural in dogs,

Human failure at forgiveness

Holds its part in human strife.

A dog's heart is your honor –

Pet him lovingly.

Walking My Dog

Footsteps returning to the past –

How many times have we walked this road?

And truly I know the ghost that lies beyond his life.

Lump in my throat,

Treasure chest in my heart,

Imagining my life without him.

Sundaes on Sundays

Humble roots, simple tastes,

Sleepwalking through a phantom culture.

I used to enjoy digging in the earth

With a shovel —

Will I reach China?

Now no place is safe.

They fingerprinted some of us kids

In case we were abducted,

Or to establish our criminal records early.

My dog is strong-willed, independent, yet loyal:

Like me.

He is a maverick, scouting frontiers,

Only to bring back order:

Like me.

Sundaes on Sundays.

The Walk

Do people search a lifelong through?

Sniffing a route,

Dog's nose to earth glued?

The first part of the walk,

I was caught up in my thoughts;

Then I started to enjoy it…

Dogs have an innocence at any age

That humans fail to reach at every age.

My Dog Life

Moving across the rugged hills of the land where I live,

I arrive at a safe valley,

Where I am protected from the threatening winds of life;

It is a secure space, secure like my childhood.

Stilling the time frame,

Taking me back to mother's hot chocolate,

My warm, wool mittens and father's securing arms --

Free-spirited and unrestrained,

Mother Nature gently swaying my fragile body in her great arms,

The rustling winds of late September bringing about sleep.

With skinned knees and a dirty face,

I explored my small and peaceful world,

Feeling free among the small plants and vast trees around me,

Forming my own small buds of knowledge daily.

As with all things, my secure childhood eroded with the cycle of nature,

Erasing the individual grains of innocence and warmth,

One by one,

Until I am left standing alone,

Exposed,

Left only with vivid memories of rich satisfaction

From my dog life,

Lovingly cuddled and free to explore without fear.

When I become my grandpa,

Like him, only me,

I'll be as young as old can be,

Sitting near a tree.

You had to navigate your whole life,

Still you think the course was wrong.

Shoes are tied and heart's beating regularly,

But the sun is pressing down.

I crashed into the sunrise,

Gave up believing in the moon.

Cheated death,

Wiggled my toes,

It's afternoon.

I'm clearing my path of the likes of you,

I have been for years.

Where I'm going is troublingly unknown,

But it's beyond your simple views.

That belly feeling,

When you're off to school;

Excited to learn,

Before college ruins it all.

Higher education:

They trained us for nothing,

And put price tags on our souls.

The baby walked to school,

Tying his shoes before.

"Two plus two equals heartache –

I'll never count that high.

They'll give me a blood bandana,

Stars dancing in the sun."

Final report card: Nowhere to report.

A bucket of empty prefixes is all it got this clown,

And now his shoes have holes.

Left-brainer!

Everywhere you turn, there are tools to support you.

Right-brainer…

Good luck!

I cannot find the glass of salts,

It troubled me to find.

It must be incidents at fault,

Where forward meets behind.

It feels different – time –

When you're older:

Less traction and faster.

Haunted closets of adult life:

Your friends are outside,

Laughing under bright lights.

Great far sky,

Hearing the clang of our mistakes.

A crumbled mass of sugars

In the middle of the night,

Rebuilding itself, by sheer will,

And opposition to decay.

Why did I pull a cloud over my head

When it wasn't even raining?

Stepping on another man's foot

While running away from myself.

That sun feels nice, wherever it's coming from.

My mind could change –

How it feels,

Never how it's designed.

Incompatible

Lay your head next to mine and rest a while.

I played it cool when my heart was on fire.

You stooped so low to elevate me,

Then broke me.

It was a spasm of the minute,

Wanting more than what we knew nothing about.

You mistook caution for lack of interest;

I mistook silence for patience.

When a woman experiences unrequited love:

"Oh, did he break your heart?"

When a man experiences unrequited love:

"Get over it! She doesn't love you!"

Wisdom of the Trees

Are we living just to feed memories to the future?

I apologize for not enjoying life sooner,

To all those affected by it.

But my dog helped me find beauty in the natural order;

He is my anchor in rough seas.

The trees are calm and cool,

And their love is magnetic.

I enjoy the tall grass by my side,

As I cycle beside it.

You haven't accepted me for who I am,

Because I haven't either.

I won't give you my attention –

You must compete with the trees.

The wind feels better at my back than at my face.

Why is that?

It is a force, like love,

Some feel safer turning their backs against.

My fantasy mind went wild as a child.

As my fantasies failed, I am forced to find positivity.

Such potential in dream kingdoms!

The enticements of childhood that grow the bones.

A meaning-speckled planet

Shakes you up and leaves you lost.

Pass the riddle of life,

Unsolved,

To the next generation.

The world sighs,

Looking at itself.

Train Ride Requiem

We wipe the snot from a million dirty faces,

Tick-tock, time goes on for some reason.

The mountains crash and tumble all around and you live to retell the boredom,

And still, time presses on.

Tick-tock.

You live longer and better and do more than you thought possible and wonder,

Is this the end?

Tick-tock.

I am so young, my options seem replete.

Is this where I choose another soul, get dusty inside,

Suffer inner defeat, or face the dawning tide?

Tick-tock.

The time shall pass,

Till you decide, or die.

Death wipes away another word defeated by the press,

In hollow syncopation, timing flavor-fueled duress.

Thank the silent prisoners, the trains dying in your throat,

The soliloquies, internment – nervous, wilted, jilted jerk.

I am a song with a voice three seas removed.

Somewhere my brethren wake and recall how I am opted sleuth,

To the world branch fire, please just leave me alone --

Can't you see I'm on internment on a solitary throne?

Made of brass and bronze and some stolen copper thrice,

Bent to silver rather sliver hinder normative device.

I keep expecting your tender heart to pass,

Through an airport made of windows down the velvet grass beneath.

Instead, I tire at the sound of hearts in beat.

Find a prison, find a throne, see a field of golden trend,

And aspire to composite every sound at quaking shore.

My confidence is shaken, I can't fool them anymore,

Nor even do I want to, for there's more of me in you.

Come, tears, come, to make me fresh and new,

Give me clearance from appearance which her eyes easily undo.

The world colossal, not so grand,

Pours the sea into your hand,

And blows a quiet whisper

'Gainst the chaos of the night.

Or the chaos of your thinking,

Splitting Normandy and Rome,

Into the logic of decision

And explosion of free mind.

Infinito motion ever, each drops from game when time.

A million wizened angels call the fright at night to rest,

Thanking grace and cheer and kindness for an end to day conquest.

With Romania at heart, one can stare into the sea,

And find a thousand children singing oracles of glee.

Infinitum never bend or break your rightful stride with friends;

As a mother hovers life, so we tend to dour life,

Episodes so clandestine, sublime cool and smooth the mind,

As it readies for completion near the end of wounded time.

Have you forgotten to do something, as did I?

Remembered, oh yes, deep inside, but courage dropped,

And up stood time to shout, "This life is grand!"

But only at those moments when objective's not at hand.

Only heard the absent humor, some tardy hard display,

Of ever-present rumors so explicit to the day,

Who waits with sunshine jeers

And a pocketful of press,

To scatter on the masses,

Emollients to duress.

Ascending my gaze

In the frontier of night,
Starchy white landscapes
Hinder my sight,
Of limitless heavens
And unearthly might –
Squinting,
Straining,
These clouds I do fight.

Whence from the sky
Dropped a threesome of birds –
The eagle,
The vulture,
And raven
Converged.
First fell the eagle,

Extended,
    Direct,
But migratory winds
Swept under his breast.

Next dropped the vulture,
Suspecting a fly,
But sterile and senile,
He beat me
To die.

Alas now, Herr Raven
(Who knows all the lies)
Perched cunningly,
Clawing,
Exchanges his eyes;
Pecking, not pleading,
The Raven and I
Depart with near misses,
And probably sigh.

Death March

Coldness surrounds absence,

Apathy intermixed,

Suspended amongst the smell –

Putrid urine and decomposing lives.

The mirror

Above

The stained wash basin –

Cracked, tarnished, dull.

The final

Sinking

Realization;

Wasted life from birth,

The anti-Darwin.

Distant footsteps

Ring

Hypnotic cadence

In the prisoner's head.

Closer,

Closer,

As the last embers --

Self-hope --

Are stamped out,

With each

Approaching

Step.

Silence.

The Grim Reaper heralds

The man,

No conscience, no forgiveness,

Extension of the hollow grip –

Clutch, not comfort --

Guiding the man

To his death march –

50 paces

Until the end.

The Chair

Shadows the Soul,

Drawing him

Closer,

Closer…

A poison

Like

A poison –

No antidote.

"The end of the line, son," announces the priest.

"No," replies the prisoner,

"Just the erasing of the graphite smudge."

Between

"This is what I set out to do"

      and

"This is what I have done"

        Lies

            The fleeting moment.

Alongside time,

We are not drivers,

But geography –

From a cloud's perspective.

Nearby time,

There is never a rhyme.

Along the Tracks

Train whistles

Attempt to conceal

Fragility –

Rusted rails,

Weeded consciousness,

Oblong heritage.

Wails brood,

Lazy links

Of the train

Passively transport

Wealth —

Other pathetic fancies —

From icehouse hearts

To crowded inventories —

Merchandise with which to love ourselves.

Degenerates line the park benches,

Businessmen and businesswomen hustle in the morning obnoxiousness,

Young precious eyes open with the rising sun,

The prison guards clang the doors of the prison cells.

Does anyone care?

No one cares.

Crawling in the unrelenting sands of time,

Searching for a haven.

Mirages of destiny,

Toying with my mind.

An oasis of confusion

Restrains me from continuing –

I am what I do not know.

The morning sleeps

In darkness

Until the insects buzz

With laughter

And it's light

Every sunrise

Is a different god

Performing a new creation.

Youth and Choice

So free to make good decisions!

Bad decisions…

An exercise of the will,

A chemical cocktail,

Exploding and burning.

I have seen it in the dance clubs,

In the automobile cocoons;

A watchful moon,

Drunk on the clever secret.

They said the smile was somewhere,

Perhaps in a forest.

It was not near the edible mushrooms,

Nor the poisonous one either.

What did the writer do before literacy?

Throw his hands in the sky?

There's a different principle at play

At lakes.

A lost ball – rocking against the shore…

Leave it for its owner to return.

Another day?

An owner with no identity,

And no fixed schedule.

Warming myself in the sun like a homeless man,

My shoulder burning from the Ph.D.

Walking with Father

The memory of your father

Jumps into your mind

Amongst an avalanche of thinking.

What brought it?

A plea for help?

A magnitude of footsteps…

Then a quick dash to the car.

A boy must put his manhood

On a shelf

Before he can become a boy again.

There's a lot of stuff you can do

That's a "waste of time."

You're more yourself

When you're less private.

42

I learned to eat an apple to the core in Russia.

I learned to bundle my scarf up to the neck in Poland.

I have walked on streets

A total stranger,

Felt the privacy

Of anonymous horror –

Yet starved within the circle.

The mind is criminal in the corner,

The heart is ragged in the wilderness.

Swimming

I could have been a great martial artist –

Swimming is my martial art.

I could have been a great musician –

Swimming is my musical instrument.

I could have died that day –

Swimming saved my life.

Spirituality is a shadow around a corner,

Which grows more elusive with age.

The trees and cubbyholes of grass are the same,

But feel less protective –

Less like a womb,

More like an alien mother.

Half-Fallen Tree --

The old, lone, half-fallen tree in the forest –

Nothing lonelier in the company of erect life

Than a half-fallen tree.

Thoughts walk around

To the worst neighborhoods in town,

Then have a meal in a good restaurant

And whistle a different tune.

Thoughts walk around

To the best restaurants in town,

Then bump into a stranger

And vomit in the gutter.

Reflections of a Failed Writer

Don't write about that, about which you don't know that much.

What do you do with the label of "writer"?

Waste a couple of decades exploring its implications?

I can't believe how much I wrote,

And how bad it was.

I gave up on myself,

Moving the pen mechanically

In a recovery process.

Threw out many treasured things,

When I couldn't find my face in a hundred clouds.

Imagine someone you greatly admire:

Would you let that person read your lines?

If not, the lines are not worth printing.

A mature writer abandons the wild misuse of fancy words and aims instead to express clever ideas using interesting language.

Meltakron

The trees move and cause the wind to blow.

The snakes congregated along the ridge, beneath which was a direct route to the sea.

The foam in the river used to just be horse spit.

To forgive is canine.

The First Glimpse of Sunrise

In the intense August heat, as the long, slow-droning solar waves strike the fields, the green, tall, uplifted, and proud corn stalks sway gently and quietly in the breeze, stretching upward toward the sun.

The dead, blank heat of day gives way to the deep calm of clear, black night. Field mice dart about the bases of the corn stalks in the dark. The cornfield bustles with nighttime activity: here a scamper, there a crunch – creatures in movement, life animating life.

Nels tended to rely on body language in most company when getting his point across. With his grandson, Nels was more talkative. Nels was a tall, lean man of Danish descent. To the young grandson at his side, Nels was larger than life. Nels blended into the landscape: a farmer with strong hands who wore faded denim; he needed a shave, but not by field standards. Nels had a feel for the soil and a knack for growing vegetables. How those hands would shovel into the loose, dark, rich, Iowa soil and make magic of a green variety. If this ground could speak, it would ask for Nels.

"Grandpa? Can I ride on your shoulders while we cross that field?"

Nels was disinclined to model an easy life to the boy by offering him a shoulder ride. The land is an inhospitable host, and there is no easy way to live with her.

Nels answered, "No, Heath. Use your young, strong legs to move yourself!"

Grandfather and grandson were returning to the grandparents' house to enjoy the meal that Grandma Mabel had just finished preparing for them.

Mabel stood in the kitchen, greeting her husband and grandson with a beaming smile animating her face. She proudly stood next to the table where the meal she had prepared for them was situated. Mabel was skilled in creating magnificent things from basic elements, such as a delicious feast from simple, wholesome ingredients. The dresses Mabel sewed for her daughters had higher design quality than most clothes sold in stores. Mabel was prolifically creative, felt great love and joy for her family, and everything she made for them possessed a special energy.

"Did you catch any fish?" Mabel asked.

"We caught a couple of sunfish," Heath replied.

"If you and Grandpa clean them, then I'll cook them for supper," Mabel offered.

Though there were chores to do, Mabel was less concerned that Nels do his chores when Heath was around. One chore that never seemed important to Mabel was sweeping and mopping the floors; the dirty floors just made the house seem more lived-in and inviting, and an indication that the grandchildren were having fun was the change in the color of the bottoms of their feet from clean pink to dirty black.

Following lunch, Nels and Heath walked to a nearby cornfield to see how high the corn was growing; harvest time was only a couple of months away. The mid-day sun blazed down. The heat was oppressive, and it slowed their pace. The sky shot forth absolute blue from halted infinity.

Reaching the side of the cornfield, they stopped, and Grandpa Nels quietly studied the corn.

"Grandpa, you must be rich to have all this corn," Heath remarked.

"Gosh no, Heath. This is not my corn. I just help grow it," Nels admitted.

The corn, now a green as sincere as life may breathe, would soon wither to yellow, surrendering its soul as life changed seasons. A great gust of wind burst through the field, igniting a sizzling applause across the endless rows of corn.

Nels beckoned his grandson nearer, so that they may both examine an ear of corn, still attached to the stalk, which Nels was holding. Heath tore off a section of husk covering the ear of corn and smooshed it in his palm. Nels tore back the husk to expose the ear.

"Old teeth," Heath remarked. "The kernels look like old people's teeth."

Nels smiled with a closed mouth. "Hmm," he muttered. "Yes, these kernels are like old teeth,

stained yellow. You could say the kernels of corn have been telling their stories for so long that it's turned their teeth yellow. Their stories are as full of meaning as any stories you'd read in books."

And now, Nels was holding the story in his hand.

"Heath, do you believe this ear of corn has a story to tell?"

Heath replied, "Maybe it's more like a work of art, and we read its meaning that way."

"I think," Nels continued, "That the story of the corn is a bit of a mystery, but the color and taste of the corn provide a vague narrative that joins our dreams and trails into our daytime thoughts. Heath, let's go down to that stream and consider what story it may be telling."

Nels and Heath tripped down a yawning hill toward a trickling stream. At the side of the stream, Nels crouched down, dipped his hand into the cold, running water, reached down into the bed of the stream and grabbed a handful of clay, bringing it above the surface of the water.

"I think," Nels continued, "That this clay, like the corn, is also telling a story, and the beauty of this story too lies in its mystery."

Nels dropped his hand back into the water, releasing the clay into a chaotic cloud. Nels removed his hand from the water; the veins on the back of his hand were sticking out from contact with the cold water.

The lines in Nels' face were quite pronounced today. He looked down at Heath.

"Any clue as to what kind of story this stream may have for us, Heath?"

Heath wasn't sure, but he found it comforting not to be able to answer.

"And yet," Nels continued, "It feels as if, deep down, we're learning something from this stream, doesn't it? It's as if we're getting wiser, more spiritually aware, just by being near it."

Heath nodded in vague understanding. Perhaps this lack of clear understanding was less a reflection of the boy's youth and more a reflection of the broader human condition as it attempts to understand the surrounding world of nature.

Years later, there is a whisper in a field, and Heath wonders if this is the voice of his grandfather, whose death preceded the moment by many seasons.

"Grandpa, are you now telling a story of the land, in the whispers of the grass, as a breeze dances across it?"

Bodies are joined as spirits across the ages, generation to generation. It is all happening beyond our understanding: the spirit of the water, the dream of a fallen father.

Is the muse the voice of your forebears and nothing more?

While it may sometimes feel as though we are stuck in one place, it may be at those times that we are standing in a circle surrounded by our ancestors, who help guide us on to the next stage of this trying life.

Nels spoke to Heath in a dream:

"Dull times often stand at the dawn of happier times."

In the shadows of nature, where each body stands alone and unknown to other bodies, a child senses the presence of a father recently deceased. There is a strong feeling in the room, the hint of speech or movement at an instant, a presence felt through belief: it is like the lesson taught by a flowing river, complex to discern but consuming the mind and powerfully mysterious. The simple ear of corn has a soul; you can feel it when you hold it in your hand. Your able body with wide eyes takes in the first glimpse of sunrise: the sunrise is beautiful, vast, quiet, and incomprehensible in its magnitude; it sustains our lives and spirits, and having it there allows us to carry on.

The End

Simion

Simion stood near the curb, waiting for a break in traffic that would allow him to cross the street. Simion raised the collar on his stained and ragged denim jacket, as a late October, chilly gust of wind penetrated his scrawny body. The youth recalled how his mother would scold him for not bundling up in such cold weather:

"You'll catch pneumonia and die!"

Simion lowered his gaze sadly.

"Dying wouldn't be such a bad thing," he thought.

As the boy hustled across the street, he coughed a few times in step.

"Hello, Simion!" shouted a voice some distance away. Ignored, the voice grew irritated: "I said *Hello*, Simion!"

Squinting in the direction of the voice, Simion caught sight of Frank, an old, local homeless man who was huddled around a barrel fire. Simion didn't like Frank, since Frank was a person, and Simion didn't like most people. Simion suddenly changed the direction he was walking so that he could create a quick distance from the man.

In this neighborhood, even the most street-savvy visitor would enter with cautious steps and shifting eyes. Simion had lived here for a while now, and he knew that danger could come from any direction; the lack of safety had hard-wired him to stay alert.

Simion was too young to be considered a man, yet too old still to be considered a boy. Simion was overdue in returning the youth he was borrowing from his past, and the looks in the eyes of his elders told him that he was not where he should be, that he was late for something undefined. The tall buildings surrounding Simion made him feel small. He made his way to the end of a damp, dirty alleyway, where lay a piece of cardboard that served as his living space. A soiled blanket lay rumpled to the side; a folded sweatshirt served as his pillow. Litter surrounded him. Simion sighed. How had he gotten here? What a boy he once was! – His family had sometimes made him feel special. His erstwhile home life had not been perfect, but he had been comfortable and not in want. Simion was quite different from his parents though, and they had difficulty raising him because of this difference. A dirty, stray cat was sitting on Simion's cardboard bed.

He pushed the animal away with his foot and sat down, dejected and tired. Simon exclaimed to himself, "Home Sweet Home," though his surroundings muted this sentiment.

The following morning, Simion awoke from a ragged sleep with the cooing of pigeons and the clickety-clack of working-class feet. He headed to The Mission, a homeless shelter where a tired soul may eat a bland meal and take a cold shower. As Simion left The Mission, filth and poverty enveloped him anew.

Simion then had the rest of the day on which to entertain himself. He kicked a pop can along, passing liquor stores, peep shows, and rat-infested tenements. Then suddenly, Simion stopped walking and stared outward in thought.

The boy stood for a moment and reflected on some aspects of his erstwhile family home life that he cherished. Then drawing his mind back to the present, he could only shake his head in disbelief at how far he had strayed from that former life. It is heartbreaking when parents don't understand a child, and they raise him in a way that only half-satisfies him; it leaves him feeling incomplete, and his family bonds in turn also feel incomplete. Youth homelessness sometimes results.

The boy's anger at himself rippled out into the world around him: toward his family, friends, strangers, and God. But Simion still missed his family. His hands were crammed in the front pockets of his jeans, and the index finger on his right hand wormed at a quarter that had been wearing through the pocket. He was saving the quarter for some moment when he had the nerve to telephone his family. He spotted a telephone booth nearby -- the time had come.

Soaring in spirit, Simion danced to the telephone booth.

With each successive ring though, his spirits faltered.

"No answer. Oh well," he sighed. "Maybe I'll try again later...or maybe I won't. Damn."

The old man took a final drag off his cigarette, dropped it, and crushed it with his foot, as if the cigarette had been the cause of his suffering, then he stepped out of the phone booth. His head dropped, and a tear rolled down his face. His feet felt heavy as he moved toward a grey and orange dusk sky.

The End

Jakob and Stephanie

"Jakob, you're a good friend, but books are better friends to me," Stephanie told Jakob.

Jakob considered Stephanie's statement for a moment. "I'd rather not compare books to friends, Stephanie. The company of books is less complicated. If a book is disappointing, it's easy to close it and stick it back on the shelf. A disappointing friendship can pull our thoughts for decades."

The two walked along, cooly satisfied by the gravity pulling their feet to the ground. Stephanie moved to face Jakob, stopped them both in their tracks, and kissed him on the lips.

"In the journey of life, books help one navigate one's course. I feel very safe in the company of books," Stephanie remarked.

Their eyes met and formed smiles, joining their bodies in a strong union in the light of the setting sun.

"We learn a lot more from gazing upon nature than we do from reading books. Wisdom gained from the observation of nature is much more profound," Jakob offered.

Now seated on a rock, Jakob's and Stephanie's lips met, as if to mark a pause in the conversation. Stephanie slid closer to Jakob and laid her left leg across Jakob's right leg. Their lips again met, hesitant, as if noticing the whisper of passion between them.

"Good books focus the mind and the best ones can even calm the soul," Stephanie suggested.

"That's true," Jakob agreed. "Learn from nature, learn from books: grand wisdom, particular wisdom."

"Of course, reading outdoors allows us to gain grand wisdom and particular wisdom simultaneously. But whether we read books outside in nature or indoors, books lead us into a world of ideas," said Stephanie.

***

Years later, long after the high ideals of youth had scattered, Jakob and Stephanie found themselves in different places in their lives. Stephanie had buckled into the system, which offered an easy ride; she had taken the high road, where the vista is broad but the vegetation is sparse. Jakob had taken his own path, which was rocky but scenic; he had taken the low road, where the terrain is rugged but the vegetation is rich.

But when the two were younger and together, it seemed that the paths they would take would be similar, since many of their ideas aligned so well. They felt part of something greater when drawn together. But in their modest and polite interaction, each only revealed and shared the parts of self that seemed to conjoin with the perceived other sufficiently enough to maintain their friendship. The private self in youth senses how some of his views differentiate him from his friends, but those views are still amorphous enough in childhood not to disrupt the affinity with friends. As our views become clearer in life as we age, our vision of self also becomes clearer, and thus the self stands in more defined contrast to the outside world of other bodies. It is the journey leading us in different directions of which we are only vaguely aware while it is happening, and only becomes clear years later in reflection once we arrive at a place of better understanding, that is most fascinating to consider; it is as if the mind is leading the present self toward some future self as values take shape, as if a higher, less conscious mental state oriented toward the future is leading a lower, present-oriented mental state.

As young adults, Jakob and Stephanie came to hold differing views on religion. Jakob's spiritual values were pagan, pantheistic, while Stephanie embraced conventional Christian values. Jakob worshipped no higher power, and he honored only the medium power of Mother Nature, a frame of thinking that Stephanie would consider but wouldn't accept.

Stephanie's Christian values were in fact so adamant as to be easily skewed. During her college studies, she redirected her worship of God to the worship of the false god Schoolmaster. Worship of Schoolmaster involved staring at one spot on a page in a book in an effort to burn a hole through the page using eyesight. This feat would be the greatest tribute to Schoolmaster, though none had ever managed to achieve it.

Burning the page using eyesight was not a prerequisite for becoming a schoolmaster, and in fact each generation saw a new crop of false gods there to guide their subjects toward the feat, pinning the devotees in their seats, mesmerized, staring at the page hour after hour for years on end.

Jakob recognized the schoolmaster to be the vilest beast to prowl the earth; their grand deceit had not cast its shadow over him. Stephanie smiled to herself, confident that her repudiation of traditional values – respect for her peers, admiration for the beauty of love – would be worth it if she could be the first to burn a hole through the page using eyesight, thus becoming the one Supreme Teacher.

The schoolmaster rewarded stock thought, and stock thinkers were his disciples.

Stephanie became a critic; Jakob remained a writer.

In the domiciles of each, books lay everywhere.

The End

Holodromes

The two had just managed to retreat into their hovel in escape from the blazing heat of nature already emerging at dawn.

Each hovel was equipped with a neuro-recalibration chair used to placate the mind, to pacify the body, and to neutralize the emotional dominance of rage, or uncoded hatred. The removal from sunlight --outdoor excursions were limited to the night, and hovels were built without windows-- had resulted in high levels of uncoded hatred in hovel dwellers, so the neuro-recalibration chair was introduced to code hatred at moderate levels, thus stabilizing the social order. The hatred drew bodies together; hatred was the basis of the social bond. But too much hatred threatened to rupture the social order, so means to regulate the hatred levels of the hovel dwellers were adopted.

There were some unauthorized bodily drives that no type of coding could suppress entirely. Even prolonged sitting in the neuro-recalibration chair could not quell the overpowering human drive to roam and collapse, roam and collapse.

Hovel dwellers found ways to relieve the soul from the assault of hatred programming. They dug underground tunnels, where they could undertake the practice of anonymous sex. This provided some relief, but the hatred programming was too entrenched. The soul was deprived of the features that define it: clarity and wonder.

Oftentimes, after seeking pleasure in the underground tunnels, when attempting to return to his or her hovel, the body would end up in the wrong person's hovel, not so much because the tunnels were disorienting in the pitch darkness, but because the hovel dweller led such a numb, bland existence that his or her sense of individual identity was lost.

The hypnotism of hatred pervaded, programmed through the whirr of the coding machines. Society was stabilized by hatred programming, but excessive hatred increased social instability; the neuro-recalibration chair was the device officially introduced to help maintain moderate levels of coded hatred, but the unauthorized practice of tunnel sex was also tolerated, as this practice also helped to maintain moderate levels of hatred in society, basically because pleasure offsets hatred. Night grub foraging was also tolerated; a body fearful of attack by night predators was preoccupied with this fear, so that this connection with nature was not relaxed thus not pleasant and therefore this type of connection with nature would not destabilize the hatred programming. Sunlight disrupted the hatred programming most effectively, which is why hovels were built without windows. The artificial darkness was terrifying to most, and the angles of the hovel's shape occur nowhere in nature, so most minds regarded the angles with trained suspicion, and these minds would not allow their bodies much rest.

But the artists were more accustomed to darkness: they were cast into the dark underground by their peers; they were allowed no place in the former above-ground social order. The artist learned to adapt to this darkness; the darkness only made the artist's intuition – already one of his strong traits – stronger. Intuition is a sense that leads a body, similar to sight. In the darkness, the artist may not see, so his intuition becomes stronger, similarly to how the other senses of a blind man are sharpened to compensate for his loss of vision. The artist learned to intuit his way in the dark aboveground and dark underground, so that he became an adept grub forager and tunnel digger.

Hypertechnology had thrown earth's magnetic forces into flux, and this disturbance had rattled the orientation of most humans. Yet the artist, cast into the underworld by society, was closer to the center of the earth, so better oriented toward it. This orientation toward the center of the earth benefited the artist in his tunnel construction. Some artists who focused on self-expression with little regard for technique burrowed tunnels directly toward the center of the earth, while artists preoccupied with technique often tunneled in dizzying circles.

The ultimate artistic gesture was to incinerate oneself by burrowing as near to the center of the earth as possible.

It was a short, miraculous life with no meaning.

The End

Water Rules

It's safer in the forest. When the winds howl and the insects buzz, you will want the containment of the forest. On the steppe, the mercenaries blink. They wait, eyes dust red, pitiless. Their leather canvas pouches contain tobacco. Horse muzzles snarl a hot froth toward a feeding hand. The night. The air moves in O-shaped syllables, embracing and shifting from partner to partner. In magic shadows, stuffed with amber, ghost elders guide the living with silent speech. A body provides a voice for the gruff command, but the command itself bears the gross gravity of a million sailors lost at sea.

The wolf den is alight with paws scampering on tree bristles. Winds shook the tiny houses in their glitter. Diamond-shaped stained glass. Teardrops, industrial mud. This erect snake counted *One, Two, Three,* standing in the bullet wind leopard grass, and the merry kids followed. On *Three* they died, on *One* they were born, on *Two* they lived. Big dragon king leered in atmospheric grey; he was knitted by slumped, maddened hands, two on zero for six trillion scattered rags of patchwork: his skin. Bracket teeth howl a lonely infinity down neglected fence lines. Water rules. A thousand dresses rustle whispers and meddlesome smiles from the clamorous assault of past pleadings to the still of the water-drenched inner ear. Bubbles ascend at a leisurely pace, while the toddler beneath words relaxes his face.

The System That Smothers the Soul

With swimming, we enjoyed the air of relaxation into our sunny lungs. We boys moved with the spirit of competition: for some of us, this came naturally; for others, the competition aligned well enough with the combat in our heads; and for others, a desire for general camaraderie with peers kept us competing.

The strong bonds of our friendships empowered us as individuals. The friendships felt strong enough to conquer any calamities, present or future. But for those of us who foolishly believed that as friends we would be there for each other for all our lives, the realities of adult life, in which childhood friendships tend to be sidelined, would prove to be disappointing.

Our bonds remained strong only within the culture of swimming. As our years of swimming together ended, the bonds collapsed and the memories withered.

My navigation of self will never again find reflection in their eyes. When we lose touch with our friends from childhood, our memories of our younger selves become muddled; the memories others hold of us inform our understanding of self.

We toned our male bodies for the ladies later to ravage them. We shone the light of friendship on each other's souls, only for the ladies later to ravage us.

It wasn't enough just to learn how to swim and to enjoy it -- we were trained to compete as a team, yet also to compete against one another. Is it any wonder then, that the friendships didn't last? Friendship and competition are disparate energy states.

Blood on my shoes, she kissed me hard.

The wild men were plundering toward the sea, never arriving, even when arriving, never realizing it was the sea they were plundering toward, the place that calmed their violent nerves.

They make you feel as though you are never good enough, no matter how hard you work: this is the design of competition, in athletics and academics; the joys of athletics and learning are hampered by the pressure to overperform. The helpless child is forced to quell the spirit of his heart. The heart is removed of its duty as captain of its ship. The growth of society depends on a body subordinate to the system. Oftentimes, those who achieve the highest success in society have abandoned core aspects of self.

Those who most sold their souls to the system became devotees to the religion of egomania, the sole preoccupation of which is that the importance of the self has a direct correlation with results on standardized tests: the higher the score, the more valuable the human. These tests, though, measure only a sliver of intelligence and aptitude, so that the belief system of this religion of egomania is fallacious, and its deleterious effect on society is far-reaching.

School submerges the psyche – the system thus is stable. Those who awaken to realize they are victims of the system find escape difficult.

A person's identity is tied to the decisions he or she makes; decisions are made within the system; the system dissolves the essence of the individual; the individual lacks his elemental sense of self when making decisions, so that his decisions, as he is a cog in the system, are poor first and improved only as he is able to distance his understanding of self and its desires from the dissonance on the soul caused by the system.

The Pen and the Fantasy Within

Perhaps someday they'll dedicate to me a nice, quiet, city park, splotched sunny, unraked in the fall. For now, I'm just a name scribbled on a picnic table frequented by teenage cigarette and beer enthusiasts.

The playful sun mixing with the shadows silhouettes a writing bench chosen. They do not seem to discriminate much, here on the park benches. We all choose our company -- mine is language. Just knowing I have writing to turn to makes me joyful; writing saves my spirit.

Spring is here and my words drift toward the sky and play in the tree tops. Spring brings fair weather, and inspiration to write follows. Clouds and sunshine intersperse, meaning the point is reached off and on. There's a looming lightness of expectancy, the intimations of spring in the artic valley. A season for poets and songbirds alike, in this country.

Thoughts such as I'm writing spring from the bushes and leap through the door. My unseen audience cheers me on at dawn, a flock of birds perched on ordinary branches. Earlier in the fall, an ecstasy overtook my hand with a pen, as I beheld trees and children in this alien land. I'll write something about the cold, I told myself, as I tripped across the icy, slick street between yellow buses and through fog to my place of rest from work.

Streaming through crowds, all those early impressions lost, I without a pen. I was roaming in thoughts across various terrains and moving my pen at the same time. My bench pushes me off to other adventures. Good writers are good thinkers. The season packs up in a hurry, the poet shakes the earth.

Penmanship and sentence formation displaced childhood too damn quickly. I expend 300,000 breaths just to glean one worthwhile expression from the cosmos, while you gobble it up in one quick snatch. Words and their meanings float in space, occasionally colliding. Your eyes will search out the cool retreat of phrases. You've got to write in the direction the language is going.

Childhood and Reflections on Childhood: The Two Stages of Life

The terrified boy caught sight of a dark-bearded man in a top hat and black cloak slipping into a side room down the hall. The boy saw the man often when the boy would make his way to the top of the stairs, and so the boy was reluctant ever to go upstairs when home alone. The boy feared the man upstairs.

A red and yellow stuffed toy dragon terrified the boy, and his sisters once tortured him by shutting him in the closet with it.

The boy had blood gush from his head cantankerously, as he stumbled into the arms of four men running to his assistance. The boy lay drenched in his precious fuel until he was whisked away to the special room where broken crowns are repaired.

The boy sometimes awakens at night and feels the presence of spirits standing next to his bed.

I was born then raised where the devils graze.

My childhood memories are strong flames that will send me right off to the market, where the screams from distant wars panic the eardrums of stall operators into buying and selling confusion. I feel as though I knew myself better as a child; adult life seems to consist of musings over the lost person known in childhood. The older we grow, the less frequently come the compliments. Leisure time is relished in childhood, but it's harder to feel at ease ever as an adult. As a child falling asleep on many nights, I envisioned that the best strategy in war is always to be on the strongest side. Fog seeps deeply into haunted youth beliefs. Childhood is repeated at the day's end, only it is slower and more aware; youth is the cloud of uncertainty and old age is the exposure of uncertainty.

Kids

Kid, you're so cute, such a sight to behold!
Take me to your leader so to never grow old.
Find a dime on the playground, make it your fiery gem,
Forts and castles netherworld, masters of stratagems.
A sob from you is like a tear in my heart,
Which drains away the trauma of a thousand Bonapartes.
An acre after till is worth much less than the clod
Trodden lightly by the kid whose world begins to flaw.

I am a traditional man,

Born at the doorstep of Hell,

A child who can't grow out of it –

Out of Hell or out of childhood?

It could be either…

Introspection

I wasn't lost, I was hiding my talent. I was looking out for myself all along; those times that seemed like points of self-destruction were times I scrambled to defend my character. I am a leader with no leadership position. Even when I don't want to talk, people interlace me with words. I sat an undervalued entity, wishing to escape to distant shores. I departed the first name basis people cluster, and headed toward a more relaxing, darker side street. I stammer about and defend my plastic physique against the monstrous norm. I feel as though I'm a puzzle piece never brought into play. I'm standing so close to me that the glare is blinding. The world pulled me up, though I did not believe in it. Usually I don't look at people, because they won't give me the looks I want. I'm always comparing myself to others, those whom fortune has wadded into a ball and placed upon a shelf. The earth rumbled, I awoke, fresh patterns on my skull. I'm trying to block the thousand screaming voices, the coaches and critics, and eat supper at my own table. Now as I sit at my writing table, I want to leave the sounds of rugs being swatted, dishes clanging, and the heavy buzz inserted into my thick-layered space. They gave me a book of fairy tales to prepare me for the nervous future. Nothing that I've found in this life seems as important as learning.

How Amazed

A symphony of emotions carves facial landscapes. Lines and crevices quietly land on our faces in the night, stealing our youth. Do not comment upon my appearance as it alters beneath a thousand cement beliefs. I rush to the mirror to chat with cancelled former faces. I stood before the mirror to make sure I was still here, not another phantom, a ghost wind hospital tossed on a breeze. I'm not a criminal when I wake up confused in the cold heat of blurry sunshine screaming through my window.

Notes from Russia

A Ferris wheel stands against the wet, pale blue sky, as worse conditions of a gloomy, harsh winter are soon to come. I just do what the calendar tells me to do, spiritually hibernate when the wind crusts flake against my cheek in the pouring coldness, the pale dryness of winter's dead heat. The extreme cold paralyzes vanity. Last night, walking along the long, white, snow-hardened paths that extended into the flat distance under the orange glow of warm street lights, I felt that everything is still exotic, and that these are absolutely the best days of my life. The late morning sun accents light from shadow on the snowy ground; I am in the company of one man stopped to hear the same spirit I had wrapped around my mind. Some may slip through the cracks, even though their warm desk lamps glow from their studies down to the beaming street slick with ice. Some stay, some go, but the floor creaks the same. The old lady reliving her youth danced alone before the red-suited musicians -- Father Frost's deputies -- and danced a crooked waltz with her invisible partner, presumably her late husband, cupped hand in hand. Winter's wisdom I promise myself to retain each year, and each year it passes with each new thaw. Our footsteps get more cautious, we don't slide across the ice when thinking about tomorrow's lecture to prepare.

The sun feels a long way off today; the white trees are padded fluffy white, bluntly glittering with hoarfrost. I returned to the park where the madness began, now a white vacancy of snow, no benches, only me.

Trees are ministers of quiet delight, coaches of mysticism. The tips of tree branches applaud the return of warm weather. Feet wait to become sloshy during spring rains. Disgruntled faces, dark and mysteriously creviced, squint at pieces of sunbeams that are trying to penetrate a sky nearly filled with clouds. A wise old man, I am not afraid to stroll in the park, to sit on park benches and witness nature passing. A black rain started to fall, and people were closing the wooden shutters on their homes; it felt like the end of the world. I make my safe passage into nowhere streets, along slick railways. Falling rain lands in puddles of gray, uncollected diamonds. Clicking heels whirl mud spatters into gross night, drab and moist. Out across the ankle-deep water, the metal swing set sat lonely along the shore. Telephone wires curtsy along the roadside, the bus hums steadily, the windows fog over regardless of season, the traveler watches the sighing of grass, asphalt, stripes of yellow paint, and a jagged horizon. I passed along the railway tracks not long ago; further on, the track complained, straight and hazy, exhaling gas fumes under the hot liquid sun.

Glistening fudge frosting sludge makes for a treacherous terrain, not at all eased by animal tranquilizers quivering the bowels and wobbling the feet. The ingredients for an American Pie were strewn haphazardly into a closet, worthless in the industrial haze of Kurgan, Russia. Our hero laughs, oozing his mind syrup through dead bolt propositions for more than lead-based borsch. Meditative floor creaks vacillate, nervously expecting to hear a satisfactory pulse within the oak electron chamber.

At night, the influx of syllables changes to a morose slide whistle romance. Near the train station, along the large, insulated heating tubes rising from the frozen, snow-covered earth, I heard the echoey voices that earlier I mistook for ghoulish psychosis flying on the air.

The past rushes forward, wisping over the brass-ivory Siberian fields. Young lovers float sideways, whispering painful somethings. Nature drip dries itself beyond the brass rail mushroom bloom.

Heavy mist near the ground cancels my shadow and buries my footprints. One face can transform one thousand nightmares into a selected phrase, as often happens on my morning walks. I chased the cloaked paranoia at walking pace through urban stretches, the beggars and panhandlers directing me where to go with jingling purses and silver tongues. The dark, mad woman with the ageless laughter sits on a bench and orchestrates shadows behind trees.

The soft rain ran long, cold yawns through humble trickles in the streets. A feeling of precious buoyancy in a blind, rich valley pierces the paralyzed shutters. The kids run the fields early in the morning, later to carry berries in buckets.

Let's take our dreams and wring the tears out, sop up the mess, and make clever girls bow their heads as we walk purposefully to have a chat with available birds. Let's expose our shifting moods, puzzle at the rest, and drink the cool mist densely carrying the forest's tongue to my windowsill.

Nimble, fiery nights help shadows tame the tremors that fracture iron might. Hesitation courts strange devils. Eyes scope out field hands refraining from dance sprees. Poverty props green shovels against warped, wooden cottages.

Our legs get stuck in the invisible sands of our stereotypes when meeting strangers. Apprehension tugs at the frail chemistry of fair tidings. Time excuses away the dry hinges from ricocheted tongues. I have an appointment to keep with nursery rhymes.

You have no ego in the field, only function.

Balancing the internal strength

With the external sickness,

I promise to spread.

Aboard the bus,

Shoulder to shoulder with the mustached soldier,

I am 150%!

Patchplay

Reflection and good decisions are the products of a relaxed, contented mind. You can have a good mind and not know how to use it. The calibration of sense to environment creates a sort of normalcy. Nerve endings are the soul's handy men. The soul is wed to the giant, frantic, amusement earth. The soul is a tiny beam of light whose very luminosity alone maintains sanity in the mind. It is not the brain as a physical organ that keeps the mind alive; it is thoughts and ideas that keep the mind alive. Meditation is the private religion of the soul; politics are the public intoxication of the mind. Capitalism is like a pet snake: when in its cage, you can show it off to your friends, but outside its cage, you're its lunch. The only things the rich have more of than the poor are delusions.

Culture is the tie that binds alien figures in space. The universal in us has vanished, which is called spirit loss. Spirits comprise the invisible order around humans. When the soul leaves the sleeping body and travels, the mind and memory must be part of it! The smartest scientist on the planet is not smarter than the earth. Earth is a product of the devil and God, as an apology, adorned it with flowers.

Real growth is realizing that along the way, you were trying to navigate the best you could with what you had going on – this realization reflects a type of trust in the judgment of one's former self. You cannot be guided or encouraged to do things your own way by people who themselves are not doing things their own way. Discontent sets our feet in motion, from the crib on up. Placement in a future vision drives labor every day. The future seduces us and the past haunts us, so we numbly exist. In this life, there isn't enough time to unravel the why fore and the how, yet still we live. The folly of the past and the obscurity of the future stabilize the present. Our lives are but flows of action remotely processed. No trend is irreversible, said the squeaky cupboard door to the hand that dared. Some bodies operate under the assumption in living that answers to the great questions shall dawn upon man. Depression is the vivid realization of mortality. Conquering gloom is a consuming goal of some lives. Understand the people and speak for them, then as such become the people -- true for all great leaders. Don't stand within a maze of thwarted enthusiasm. There's only one shot at this life, which explains both reservation and abandonment. To live in fear is to live in the shadow of potential. I wonder how much guidance comes through eye directives from strangers. Meet each pair of eyes, and the war with the masses lessens. Inequality is a source of conflict. The conversation stands as a declaration of our being lost. If you want to prepare and plan for the long run, you must run for a long time. Defy nitwits who find comfort in uniform feeling. We reassert our identity at the most crucial of times. Stop kicking yourself over your decisions that ended up being in your best interest; you were just reacting to others groaning from their dark places. It's not what you do, it's where you are. Lost is a monster of direction.

Baby Loves Magic

In sixth-grade, I had a teacher who first took notice of my talent for writing. This teacher, around seventy years of age when I was one of her pupils, was strict, feared by the younger pupils who would have her as their teacher when they would become sixth-graders. With a shawl draped over her shoulders, she monitored the classroom with authority and discipline. This teacher was a strong, early mentor to me in my interest in creative writing. At our parent-teacher conference, in her stern, elderly voice, my teacher shared with my mother her opinion of my writing talent: "He has a gift."

Creative writing is my vocation, and this vocation was evident to me from an early age, at a time when many of my classmates likely did not know what their vocations may be; some of those classmates likely still do not know. A vocation in the creative arts, however, seldom materializes into a career. Those who fail to identify a vocation at an early age often surpass in their career developments the creative types who identify vocations in early childhood. Because nurturing the talents of creative people is not typical practice in society and the general educational system (though society gluttons itself on finished creative works), there often arises neither a clear career path nor a general future placement for the creative person. Because the creative person is independently-minded, the lack of specific, clear, career pathways for him only challenges him to utilize his strengths in self-navigation to create alternative ways of making a living.

I prefer to consider myself an artistic writer rather than a creative writer, since I consider poems and short stories -- types of writing I do -- to be art forms. An artist is not exclusively someone who paints or draws creatively; all forms of creativity are art forms. So, the term "art" should not be limited to creative drawing or painting, but should include all forms of creativity, whatever the medium.

An artistic writer in a good frame of mind writes about nature, for example in the lines "the moon drifts lonely," and "a gently caressing, playful breeze excites the trees." In the field of music, song lyrics not mentioning nature or not mentioning feelings relating to the perception of nature were not written by an artist in a good frame of mind. In a bad frame of mind, an artist will write of negative forces at work. Does the artist suffer from a hot temper? Then the artist is out of harmony with his environment (i.e., out of touch with nature). Does the artist exhibit traits of a powerful healer, sympathetic, a bringer of calm, warm feelings? Then the artist is in harmony with his environment (i.e., in tune with the world of nature around him).

The artist's frame of mind when he is working on a piece of art affects the quality and energy of the piece. I do not believe that art is something that can be done successfully on a 9-to-5 basis. The artist should work to attain balance in his disposition before attempting to work on a piece of art; he should be in a good, sound frame of mind – and he can feel when it is time – before working on a piece of art. No artist is inspired artistically all of the time, no matter the degree of technical training, one's sense of self, or the effort put into the field. Successful artistic execution arises from inspiration, a temporary and fleeting state of mind and spirit; the knack is to be able to accept when the moment has passed and to cease work beforehand.

Many artists still enchanted by youthful optimism may have hopes and expectations in the backs of their minds that society will support them as artists, but eventually the artist realizes that this will not happen; society doesn't take care of its artists. Art generates morale in society -- due to this significant role the artist plays in generating morale in society, people comprising society should support artists as people, rather than just consume their creations, for it is artists who nourish the health of society through their creations. Gaze upon a fantastic painting in a museum and you will be benefitted spiritually by its healing power. The artist is an odd sort, largely rejected by society, for he creates, forges ahead, treads a new path, and this puzzles many who misinterpret this journey on an independent course as the artist being lost. Or perhaps those times when it seems that the artist is lost are times when he isn't applying his energy toward his primary objective in life: to create.

It's a quick, disposable market for written artistic works; a reader zips through the words, as if the words comprise ordinary information in the perceptual field. So, in order for the writer to feel valued for his work commensurate with all of the effort he has put into his writings, a large audience must be reached; the artist should not expect a smaller audience to consider the work carefully, slowly, and repeatedly. What is it that causes a work of art in any medium to appeal to the perceiver? The arrangement of words must grab the reader; the painting in a gallery should stop the gallery visitor in his tracks. There are different means to gain the attention of the perceiver of art, but in my opinion, technique is not the principal means, and moreover, technique is of secondary importance in art. I would rather look at primitive art that is powerful and moving than at a technically refined work that lacks depth of meaning and expression.

How much time will any given viewer spend looking at a work of art? The longer the viewer looks at a work of art, the greater the impact the work of art is having on the viewer. An art enthusiast may believe, without challenging this belief in himself, that he dislikes a particular piece of art, even though he spends more time looking at that work than at another work that he believes he likes; the former work of art, though, clearly is having more of an effect on the viewer's senses, since it holds his attention longer. Adult representatives of society orient children to choose their likes and dislikes from an early age, and these preferences have their place in the world, but being made to feel from a young age that we must choose "favorites" – especially favorite colors – seems problematic. As a child, one may enjoy looking at different colors, as the sight of them evokes certain feelings and associations, but then the child is asked by an elder, "What's your favorite color?" and then the child understands that he must choose a favorite, when a ranking of favorites may never have occurred to the child beforehand. So now that one must declare a favorite color, this somehow renders the other colors less significant, and further damaging to the spirit is the fact that a part of one's profile as a person includes one's favorite color.

Mediocre artistic talents with sufficient financial and social support within the industry can achieve success; this type, sadly, tends to dominate the market. Fans of popular music especially latch on to the works presented to them, these fans not challenging themselves to consider whether they actually enjoy the products brought to their senses in mass supply. Strong business or self-promotion skills combined with less artistic talent seems be the formula for success in the popular music industry. In any medium of modern art, fame attained from mediocre work may characterize the success of the artist not due to his lack of inherent talent, but rather because the quality of his work has been debased due to the influence of his fans, whose influence on his work he has difficulty suppressing so that his individual expression may flourish. Even a highly talented artist may create mediocre work under the influence of fame: his frame of mind may feel constrained by his fans' expectations, and the quality of his art thus suffering under pressure from an audience may be less reflective of a quality of work the artist is truly capable of.

An artist, the creative person, is dominant in his right brain; dominant left-brained thinkers are not suited for the arts. Western societies slot dominant left-brained thinkers into the fields of medicine and law. However, certain dominant, right-brained, creative thinkers are suited for the fields of medicine and law in ways that Western society doesn't appreciate. The dominant right-brained thinker tends to be more spiritual than the left-brained thinker. Spiritual health is the deepest layer of all forms of health, and certain right-brained types are more in tune with spiritual health. When the dominant right-brained thinker is one who has an INFP personality type – Introverted, Intuitive, Feeling, Perceiving – he is ideally suited as a healer: harmony is at the basis of how the INFP views the world; he is oriented toward harmony (and lack thereof), and being deeply intuitive of how another body is feeling, he senses imbalance in physical health and is naturally inclined toward restoring harmony in the body. This right-brained spiritualist is an ideal, holistic healer, the medicine man of the tribe; strong skills in the arts and healing are intertwined within one personality type, the right-brained INFP; thus oriented toward spirituality, he addresses issues with spiritual health, spiritual health being fundamental to all physical health concerns. The INFP also brings out the best in others, in particular the vulnerable, which also has a healing application. The healing ability of the right-brained INFP can even be manifested in singing: a good singer heals others spiritually with his voice; singing can serve as a vocal administration of spiritual healing. The dominant left-brained, logical mind, however, sees only the step-by-step, not the big picture, so that understanding the health of a patient holistically – i.e., seeing the big picture of a patient's health -- is not a strength of the logical mind; this is relevant, because it is the dominant left-brained thinker exclusively who practices Western medicine.

Being highly intuitive, reading between the lines, seeing the big picture: again, these are strong traits of the right-brained INFP personality type. These traits also would be well-applied to the practice of law: the INFP with his strong intuition may sense the guilt or innocence of a party, and a case is built from there, if the facts lead toward an establishment of guilt or innocence; because the right-brained INFP may read between the lines, he may prove innocence or guilt more expeditiously than the dominant left-brained thinker. As long as a line of argumentation is coherent it needn't be logical. Strong intuition would have high value as a basis for the types of arguments made in legal cases. But strong intuition is not a trait of the left-brained, logical mind, who is considered exclusively to be ideally suited for the practice of law. One's score on the LSAT, the examination that tests logical thinking skills, is a primary test result considered in selecting applicants for law school. But again, a persuasive, coherent argument – in this case, in a legal context -- may be made that is not based on logic. The right-brained INFP type may intuit the innocence or guilt of a party, similarly to how the INFP is able to sense health problems in the body, as both determinations tap into the INFP's strong orientation toward harmony (and lack thereof): a criminal is not in harmony with his environment; a social nexus is out of order when an innocent person is wrongly accused.

Employment imbalances in the fields of medicine and law stem from an exclusive fixation on those with strongly logical minds being educated and placed in these two fields. The labor market at large suffers from having the wrong people placed in the wrong occupations, which metastasizes the hiring and firing cycle, while the ideal candidate often is never given an interview initially. The INFP excels at placing the right person in a field of employment, and he is adept at reshuffling workers within an organization to positions for which these workers are ideally suited, but this strength of the creative INFP also tends to be undervalued.

So, this is the pattern as I see it, and have experienced it, in society: the artist is cast aside, not celebrated until famous, not considered for how his talent may be applied in other fields. In my case, all I have is my creativity – it is my sole realm of self-affirmation in an adult life characterized by a lack of any type of career success. But fortunately, I have been able to do plenty of reading and thinking about what makes an artist tick, and as I am an artist, about what makes me tick. Musician is the career for which I am most suited, according to how I tested for career suitability based on personality type, and knowing that I'm suited to be a musician has given me more confidence as a singer: I don't feel as though I need to prove to anyone that I'm a singer. A person with a strong sense of himself as a singer does not feel that his identity as a singer is contingent upon training or popularity. Being trained for technical refinement in using one's voice for singing does not constitute the exclusive framework for being a skilled singer. I hear singers doing all sorts of carnival acts with their voices and I think, "You're already a singer, stop trying to sing!" If a person has a personality type that suits him for singing, the key to being a better singer, a better expressor of feeling with one's voice, is to condition better one's sense of self; technique is vastly secondary. Fancy or plain, a singer's natural voice has a striking effect. There is a marriage of technique and sonorous expression, but the latter, sonorous expression, may suffice for the essence of singing, whereas technique is pretty frill around the corners; technique is not a strong basis for compelling self-expression using one's voice.

An American Liberal Arts Education: Your Key to an Unhappy Life

I chose to be an English major in college in the early 1990s, as I believed that this major was the best choice for me as a creative writer; I loosely believed that my own writing abilities would improve by reading the works of great writers, and by writing essays about the works of such writers. In America in the early 1990s, a high standard of living, a light-hearted culture, and a healthy political system made life feel like a fantasy world in which one's future security seemed without question, so that study in the humanities, with its emphasis on nurturing soft skills, would not be imagined at the time to be detrimental to future career success.

I felt no urgency to plan a career. Being independently minded, I preferred to set my own course, so that I managed – somewhat rockily -- through self-guidance; this approach benefitted me in some ways, as it offset the lack of meaningful mentorship I was offered in junior high, high school, and college. This lack of mentorship extended even into graduate school: when a professor who agreed to be my advisor upon my entry into a graduate program in which she taught took one look at me when I first walked into her office, she made up her mind that she wasn't going to work with me. I'm not sure what triggered her attitude – perhaps it was just that her polarization about people was so pronounced that she immediately sorted those who fell either inside or outside of her graces. (I was so relieved when she took a job at another university, so that I didn't have to worry about having her on my exam committee!)

Though I had a strong sense of myself as a creative writer when entering college, I wore this pride and projected it against English professors in my program, who, I felt, were only English professors, lecturing about other people's literary works, because these professors lacked sufficient talent to become novelists or poets themselves.

The surface veneer of the private, liberal arts college I attended was one of celebrating diversity and forging well-roundedness. My opinion of a liberal arts education is that it twirls a body into circles so that when leaving the institution, the dizzy body whose sense of self has been scrambled must find itself anew in the outside world. You get lost, plagued with an overly broad view of the world, then you are left to try to figure out how to apply those vague skills gained from a liberal arts education. This experiment with the weak hypothesis didn't produce a good outcome in my case. It can take decades before one rediscovers who one comfortably knew oneself to be before entering an American college liberal arts program.

The tremendous work load of the college I attended, which dwarfed the light load of schoolwork that typified my K-12 education -- I actually requested homework from my 5th-grade teacher, because we were rarely given any -- demotivated me. Highly-competitive academia does not suit certain personality types, especially those demotivated by competition, and this represents a flaw in college culture. Early education pits peer against peer in a competitive environment, which eventually demotivates those averse to competition. Such a demanding work load for young adults new to college, away from home for the first time, seems excessive. College students gravitate to their peers for comfort in this radical separation from their home lives under the roofs of their parents, bonded to their siblings; if a college party scene, where peer-to-peer interaction is prime, draws many students from their studies, it should not come as a surprise.

As I graduated with degrees in English and Russian, I was just another humanities graduate left to believe that with my clever mind, I could discover a unique path with this liberal arts education. Perhaps when conferring bachelor degrees, the liberal arts programs in U.S. universities should attach the following note to the graduate's diploma: *Good luck finding something to do with this useless degree!* Liberal arts colleges function poorly, as lack of direction causes the system to move in circles: administrators and professors are misguided in their should-be roles as mentors, and students feel lost for a clear way forward. Where are these adults leading students, these "mentors"? The adult educators don't have a vision or plan as to where these educations may lead students, besides into a mush pile of enrichment.

If American liberal arts college programs cannot provide statistics that show that a certain percentage of former students of these programs have obtained employment directly related to the programs, then the programs should be eliminated altogether. The focus on developing soft skills in a liberal arts education is a flimsy cover excuse for not offering concrete vocational preparation for students beyond graduation. All forms of education should be based around vocational guidance. I dismiss the value of developing soft skills, but even in this area I experienced no meaningful guidance in my liberal arts education. At small, private, liberal arts colleges, such as the one I attended, where lack of student support can be substantial despite the low student-to-teacher ratio, there should be committees set up so that when students show poor grades, the professors of those students are brought before committees and the professors are required to explain why they are failing to ensure that the students are living up to their potentials. The students, through their parents mainly, are paying for their educations, and it is the professors who collect a salary that draws in part from tuition payments, so it should be regarded that the professors and administrators work for the students, not the other way around. Professors should be made to feel the heat for the underperformance of students in their classes.

College for me was an overpriced, poor investment. I felt guilty about how hard my mom worked to send me to an expensive party school, or as I heard it described, "A place where smart kids go to do drugs." Getting intoxicated was my self-destructive non-escape from the excessive academic rigor of my college, a gutless coping strategy shared by a number of my classmates. I partied to escape the pain I felt, brought on by poor guidance and harsh criticism from my English professors; this poor treatment by my professors toward me was brought on by my rebelliousness. My goal of strengthening my creative writing talent in college by pursuing an English major was far from achieved; you have to have confidence in your abilities in order to really shine at them, but I lost a lot of confidence due to this college's demoralizing environment. My college experience was vastly different from what I should have expected; the college environment I experienced felt cold and clinical, uncaring and cutthroat. This was a shocking contrast to all of my education leading up to college, as before college, I was accustomed to being treated kindly by most of my teachers, and although the majority of the teachers I had before entering college offered no significant guidance either, I experienced the most meaningful guidance of my entire education from my 6th-grade teacher, whose identification and recognition of my talent for writing fostered my strong belief in and commitment to this vocation.

Because my personality type is demotivated by competition, I felt overwhelmed in the highly competitive academic environment of the college I attended as an undergraduate, and I opted not to deal with the academic pressure as much as possible while still getting through, so I joined the ranks of other academic overwork escapees who sought comfort in intoxication. Again, academic life is structured to favor those students who are motivated by competition, and to disfavor those students who are demotivated by competition; the unstated assumption is that the former, the highly competitive, are better people, when in fact the academically competitive student may be driven by the social vice of self-centered ambition, while those demotivated by competition may prefer instead collaboration, collaboration reflecting the social virtue of interest in engaging with others.

My years in college were a dark time, a time when I let myself down, when I lost much interest and focus in academics. So graduate school was the time when I wanted to prove to myself that I could be a good student again, and it was a costly lesson to prove to myself, as overall, with all of my higher education, in student loans I owe an amount equivalent to the value of a small, decent, middle-income home in America. Again, I had no substantial mentorship in the small, private, liberal arts university that I attended. No one singled me out to build me up, to inspire me, to help me find and capitalize on my strengths, a type of help a student should assume he would receive, considering the high cost of tuition and the low student-to-teacher ratio.

At this overpriced, overrated, liberal arts college, the professors indeed weren't focused on helping each and every student. A fellow English major at this university once went to see a professor during his office hours in order to get help with writing a paper, and this professor told her, "Basically, your problem is that you can't write." She would have been better off not seeking any help at all. Another student I knew, who attempted to escape the academic pressures by getting intoxicated, was failing a class, but he showed up to the final exam, in an effort to show his earnestness in passing despite his poor performance that semester. Perhaps this student knew he would fail, but he wanted to demonstrate what he had learned anyway. The professor came by this student's desk and told the student that he needn't bother taking the exam (meaning because he would fail anyway). The greatest outrage I heard about at this university was that a student was given an "F-minus minus" for a grade. Really, isn't an "F" enough? Perhaps some of such professors generally lack social skills, which benefitted them as students, since they were so unlikeable that no one wanted to be friends with them, so that social life on campus wasn't a distraction and they could focus on and excel at their academic performance; friends didn't stand in the way of their ultra-competitive drives. Another reason why the liberal arts professor may be irritable is because deep down, he/she is mad at him/herself that he/she is leading students toward a dead end, as there are no jobs in the fields. Because they know that most programs of a liberal arts education are worthless, lacking vocational orientations, professors and administrators feel guilty about misleading students, but they too are caught in the system, so the only outlet is for them to inflect punishment on students, to demoralize them. Not one of my former graduate school professors has inquired whether I found a job in the field; vocational guidance for students is not the reason why they chose their professions.

While I was writing my dissertation, my father died, and around that time, either after he died or while he was dying, I taught a lesson that was observed by a professor, and this hot-headed professor who didn't like how I taught the class started screaming at me during my evaluation in his office. I broke down crying, explaining my concerns about my father, and unsympathetic, the professor asked, "Should I leave the room until you can get yourself together?"

A more efficient and valuable liberal arts education would be limited to one or two years, according to which, students are shown methods for conducting research and are shown ways to build skills in essay-writing in conjunction with this research. The idea should be that people can quickly be shown ways to study independently; learning to write for some people is a private undertaking anyway – I certainly never learned anything from written feedback on essays that I submitted.

Red ink scribbled by professors onto the essays I submitted was not something I cared to read; I was too afraid of the criticism. Late in high school and then in college, I began essay writing, but I mostly taught myself how to refine my essay-writing skills. I believe that a student should submit an essay for evaluation by the professor, certainly. Once the professor has read the essay, the student and professor should meet to discuss the essay (taking advantage of the low student-to-teacher ratio). The professor should ask the student questions relating to the essay such as, *What do you think are the strengths and weaknesses of your essay?* Following this discussion, the professor sits alone and writes comments on the essay in blue or black ink, without assigning a grade. The student is asked to read the comments, and drawing ideas also from the conversation that took place, the student makes revisions to his or her essay. The revised essay is submitted again to the professor, who writes a list of pros and cons of the essay, and to ensure that the student reads the professor's comments, the student makes a response in writing to these comments, in which the student may be allowed to disagree (in fact, he or she should be encouraged to disagree, as this is an effective means of building critical thinking skills). Then that's it: the professor records a grade in a book, and the student doesn't learn what grade he or she receives until the end of the course. This should reduce student demotivation and stress. A liberal arts education should be a pleasant experience; the optimal learning environment is one in which students are enjoying themselves.

There should be a reduction in the amount of reading required, especially for first- and second-year undergraduates. Though technically adults, college students know little of the adult life that awaits them, so they're mostly drawing on experience from their childhood upbringings to adjust to a new environment away from home; this transition requires a great deal of peer-to-peer interaction, which is hindered by a massive reading load. If there is going to be four-year college, then the first year should principally be focused on helping students to identify their personality types, and for the students to explore career options best suited for their personality types; this could serve as a basis for dividing up the student body into groups, small peer groups of the same personality type exploring possible future career paths together. A long-term consequence of this approach would be a lower turnover rate in the job market, as students have a stronger sense of those professions for which they're most suited, and so are more likely to stay in those fields and not leave jobs as frequently.

The GRE exam puts those test takers who process information a certain way at an advantage; these exam results relating to preparation for graduate studies are misleading. Different personality types process information differently. Students who excel on standardized exams such as the GRE may merely be good at following routinized courses of thought, so that they can follow an argument laid out and answer well the accompanying multiple-choice questions; such students may not be highly imaginative, not occupied with original, complex thought. Those students whose thought processes are imaginative, original, and complex may not perform as well on the GRE; moreover, such students may be misunderstood as having distracted thinking or being inattentive. Of course, it's the logical ones who are the best test takers: they have their blinders on, processing step-by-step the words in front of them only. If one feels unfairly ranked, slotted beneath those who are not as smart, or one feels frustrated because others are higher placed, he or she should keep in mind that his or her concerns probably have merit, so then he or she should be more determined to disregard the flawed system, to see through the variables that acted against him or her. In general there are too many variables at play in one's education: mentorship throughout one's schooling, home issues, belief in self, willingness to engage, and tolerance of authority; there's always more to the story regarding where one is ranked.

My personality type enjoys learning for the sake of learning, and because of my passion for studying languages, I was able to commit to ten years of graduate school. I told myself I'd figure out what I wanted to do once I completed my degree; I was sure there would be opportunities, but I was too busy to think of that while studying. When I completed my doctorate, I found data a few years old that gave the number of people who graduated nationwide for that year with Ph.Ds. in Slavic Linguistics as 35 for the entire United States; by the time I graduated, that number was likely quite lower than 35, as the field was in severe decline by that point. One may think I would be in high demand, with so few people holding my degree. But that is not the case: no one is getting the degree I got because there is nothing to do with it. My doctoral advisor actually tried to convince me to quit my program when I was about ¾ of the way through with it. He asked me, "What are you going to do with it?" This is a question that should be asked by program developers within a university, and if there is no good answer as to what a student is going to do with a degree, then the program should not exist; the weight of this problem should not fall on the student eager to learn, who naively assumes that there must be opportunities following graduation, otherwise the program would not be offered. Working through a doctoral program benefitted me in only two ways: firstly, I learned that I am able to master many topics, in areas in which I have strengths, on my own, by reading about them a great deal for a long time; and secondly, I learned how to organize in writing large amounts of information, but this I figured out on my own under the pressure to have to do so.

Some would raise the following objection: you brought this on yourself, you knew what you were doing, borrowing that money for undergraduate and graduate studies. Technically, at age 18, one is an adult, but earliest adulthood does not have prior adult experiences to reflect on. When it's a sunny day, and you're sitting in a stuffy office listening to a boring explanation of loan repayment, and all you want to do is go outside and have fun, it's hard to take the matter seriously, especially when repayment is in the far-off future. It's a stretch to argue that professors and academic administrators want to ruin students' lives at liberal arts colleges, but this almost seems to be accepted as a necessary by-product of a liberal arts educational system typified by worthless degrees and sky-high tuition.

I am one of millions of people who have fallen victim to the scam of a liberal arts education in America. There may be a day when future generations look back on the plight of American student loan debtors in the 21st-century as a grotesque reality, especially grotesque in how most of society looked away from the problem, similarly to how in England during the 18th-century, the overwork of children in horrid conditions to the point of disfigurement was tolerated -- though there were those who objected to it, just as now with widespread student loan debt: tolerated largely, with some voices objecting. The disfigured child laborers of 18th-century England had their lives ruined, as student loan debt ruins lives in different ways in 21st-century America.

Traveling to Storyland

While your sense of self may seem strong before you travel outside of your home country, once your ears hear the sounds of strange tongues speaking, your nose is struck by clues that only increase the mystery, and your eyes can't blink themselves back to common sights, that sense of self ends up as puzzled as the other five senses in the foreign environment. The body copes by constructing an understanding from the stimuli it receives, but because the stimuli are novel, the understanding is incomplete, so that coping in the new terrain can be challenging. Yet global travel broadens one's perspective: you see the same types of situations that we all must deal with being handled in a number of ways in different parts of the world, so that, if you incorporate these new-to-you models of problem solving into your own problem-solving skill set, you may grow as a global citizen to consider matters from different angles and with more dimension than your former, provincial self would have. Globalism gained is provincialism lost.

But while global travel attunes the mind toward broader, more dimensional perspectives on situations, situations are dealt with through language, so that gains made toward broader perspectives are handicapped by linguistic limitations when the traveler lacks a proficiency in the local language to be used in addressing those matters. But the use of body language, the main means of communication, can serve to offset the linguistic deficit. In Russia, one of my home-stay hosts complemented me on my ability to speak Gypsy, by which I believe he meant that I was able to work around shortcomings in my knowledge of the Russian language in order to get my point across satisfactorily; he probably had tuned into my ability to communicate effectively through my often telling silence.

As body language is the primary means of creature communication, the traveler should maximize on the use of body language in the foreign field. Verbal communication represents only a sliver of human communication, and a fixation on verbal communication as a means to get one's point across in the foreign field is disempowering. The traveler may consider at times embellishing body language for theatrical effect, in order to really stand out, to get one's point across by overemphasizing the point through body language, similarly to how in silent films, actors overperformed to compensate for the absence of the sounds of their voices as the means for getting their points across.

In Russia, over time I came to the view that, as a foreigner, I could either settle for being 50% of myself in line with how I thought Russians perceived me, or I could elevate my sense of self to 150%, adopting an attitude of superiority rather than inferiority as a foreigner – it was a matter of one or the other, as I saw it. But my personality type prefers relations that are egalitarian, so it was unnatural for me to sustain an air of superiority; this reimagining of my sense of self occurred as I was growing away from my fear of being identified as a foreigner, a fear that made me reluctant to speak Russian, because as soon as I spoke, I would be identified as a foreigner. Being a shy introvert, I wilted under the psychological weight of a foreigner complex; I feigned some extroversion as a way of contriving a stronger version of me, and this increased my feeling of harmony when functioning in that environment. Also, I learned to live with my fear of making grammatical errors in the Russian language by treating the Russian language as a tool I could use to bludgeon the subordinate, foreigner identity that was floating in my head. By forcing myself to take more chances with the Russian language, I did indeed feel myself integrating more deeply into Russian society. The nervousness felt speaking a foreign language has an interesting counterpart in the nervousness felt by the local resident when that person hears and tries to make sense of his language being spoken by a foreigner. Communication between a foreigner and a local has a destabilizing effect on both parties, and understanding this helped me to overcome some of my fear of speaking Russian; I felt less awkward knowing I was not the only awkward figure in the exchange. I became fluent, and spoke with high accuracy when discussing common topics, but when it came time to describe some activity or event for the first time, I was then required to apply the complex rules of Russian grammar to less frequently used vocabulary and to guess on appropriate collocations; at these moments, my real-time fluency decreased -- this happens with all speakers of foreign languages. This is the messy work of foreign language acquisition: many mistakes will be made, and the speaker will embarrass himself, but the speaker must be tough and appreciate the fact that locals will respect him for trying to speak their language and they will shun him for staying silent.

One time in Norway, I beckoned a horse to me by clapping and shouting out to the horse in my native language of English. The horse, correctly interpreting my body language and verbal beckoning, came padding across the field to greet me at the fence. This horse understood me with my foreign body language and foreign speech; he also understood that I am an animal lover. As a foreigner in unfamiliar lands, I found communication with local humans to be trickier: perhaps this was because humans can make an art form of putting up barriers against other humans, for whatever reasons. Perhaps at times, we just don't want to understand one another, while at other times we do. When we want to understand one another, human to human, understanding is nearly automatic, with language or without language, and at such times, we behave with confidence in our animalism, just like the horse who came to greet me at the edge of its pasture in Norway.

The crowds of people in Venice, Italy, correctly interpreted the body language I displayed publicly as I walked around their city, sobbing. My sobbing, while walking the streets of Venice by myself, was brought on as a reaction to the beauty of the place. This continued for hours. Eventually I sat down in a public square, where many other people were gathered, and I continued to sob there. Like the horse in Norway making sense of my behavior and sound, enough of these Italians may have rightly perceived my tears to have resulted from the effect the beauty of the place was having on me -- that, combined with unrelated, intense but purifying emotion that arose within me in this alien place. I didn't feel pressured by the locals to leave the square; these people found my emotional display to be acceptable, I sensed, and I feel strongly that I correctly interpreted their regard to me. Is it not a condition of the real world that a silent pressure to leave a place is a type of energy a group of people are able to project toward an unwelcome outside other? Is this energy of rejection not powerful enough to drive off that body? It seems that typically a body sensitive enough to such feelings of others, who is considerate of these feelings and attitudes, will bow out to this pressure.

I carry the role of an outsider everywhere I go, so it makes sense that I would feel comfortable in the highly salient outsider role of traveler in a foreign country. My limited grasp of the linguistic and cultural information in a place foreign to me that I visited sometimes made decoding situations there a challenge. How successfully I read between the lines varied from situation to situation.

Reading between the lines was a challenge once when it came to determining how much my safety was in question with the Russian, a butcher by profession, who was flailing dangerously across from me in our shared train cabin late one night as we travelled across Germany. This man's dance of madness was a strange display of body language. We commonly speak of a man out of his mind, but when a case is witnessed in real life, we may change our minds to the view that he should not be described as being out of his mind, but rather, that his mind is out of him.

This Russian butcher – he proudly proclaimed his profession to me at one point during his antics -- was a big, burly man. He would gesticulate the action of injecting a syringe into the bend of his arm, exclaiming, *Keefer! Keefer!* (slang for "narcotics" in some parts of Europe). The man would then fall hard back down on to his long seat, but in a moment he would reawaken in a startle with his arms flailing, looking totally dazed, then as quickly he would fall back down and return to his slumber. In that tiny cabin space, alone in the dark with this man, with no hope at this late hour for a conductor to come by to check tickets (the presence of whom would bring some feeling of security), I kept my eyes pinned on the frightening man with the desperate mind that was cannibalizing itself. He burst onto my side of our small cabin a time or two more before crashing back onto his side of the cabin in some deep state resembling sleep. No people were about in the corridor, as most passengers on the train were asleep. The passing landscape was asleep. My wakefulness felt all the more pronounced. I cannot attribute the safety that shielded me for the duration of this trip to any specific forces.

The world traveler puts himself in situations where the unfolding of events around him may be confusing, and it may be difficult to predict how those events will develop further. The mind does its best to create a normal picture out of what the mind knows to be relatively irregular. The mind likes this excitement – perhaps the mind craves the learning value from the rich source of stimuli of the exotic. The mind, thrilled by the global travel experience, insists that the body continue to partake of other such global travel adventures. The more exotic the culture, the more enhanced the mental experience. I could never have anticipated before going to Russia for the first time how exotic the country would seem to me.

Russia

Our plane dropped several hundred feet in mid-air; panic shot out of my body, as I feared that the engines of the plane had failed. I gripped the armrests of my plane seat. The plane leveled, but it then dropped hundreds of feet again -- this triggered a panic episode nearly equaling my first. The Russian pilot's descent in a stairstep fashion was nothing unusual by Russian standards, but to me it felt like engine failure causing an uncontrollable plunge, which leveled, then repeated. This would be the first of many experiences in Russia to scramble my senses.

My group of American teenage tourists had a tour coordinator who was drawn to the company of rich men. She found for herself in one hotel a Georgian prince with whom she could latch arms. The prince gave me a platinum necklace as a gesture of friendship. I unintentionally left this platinum necklace on the nightstand next to my hotel bed in my rush to pack up and leave the hotel room the next morning after I overslept.

In the summer of 1990, when as an 18-year-old I was first there, Russia was still the mother nation of the Soviet Union, though within a matter of months, the Soviet Union would cease to exist. The Russian youths with whom my American travel group made contact were eager to get acquainted with their age sakes from free, capitalist America. A common yearning among Russians on the eve of the collapse of the Soviet Union was to transition to an American-style, free-market system, and to abandon the stagnant, centralized, Soviet state economy. Long lines of people stretched down the sidewalks in front of Russian stores, where shoppers would buy whatever sometimes odd goods were available amongst the many shortages. We Americans were greeted like celebrities by young Russians when we entered Red Square; they flocked to us to trade their cool stuff for our cool stuff. These trades were being made on the black market, but we were just dealing in trinkets, so it wasn't that big of a deal. Anyway, the Soviet system was rapidly collapsing, and market control was weak, so the black market was by this point more grey in color; grey, but still the black market, and still officially illegal, though the unofficial tolerance was clearly dominant.

You always remember your first black market trade: mine was with a young Russian woman who had an amber necklace, comprised of large, beautiful chunks of the golden resin clustered all along the length of the necklace. Learning of my interest in obtaining an amber necklace, she invited me into a ladies' public restroom in order to exchange her necklace for my five U.S. dollars. My next trade lacked the level of discreetness of my first trade: two young Russian males about my age connected with me for a trade on the street. One of the young men served as the trader, and his partner took the role of the lookout. The two men showed me a beautiful, hand-painted, black lacquer box that they were offering to trade to me. They had me go up to my hotel room to get some of my personal belongings as trade for their beautiful, colorful, black lacquer box, which featured hand-painted, traditional scenes on the lid and sides. With my backpack crammed full of the items I selected in a rush, I returned back outside behind the hotel to meet the traders. (Russians were not allowed to go above the first floor of international tourist hotels in 1990.) The items I brought down for trade comprised a couple of pairs of Levi's jeans, headphones, AA batteries, a sweatshirt, and perhaps a small item or two more. The traders regarded this assortment of common American items as a fair trade for their beautifully hand-painted, black lacquer box, a type that in a retail shop in the U.S. at the time sold for hundreds of dollars. All of a sudden, our lookout alerted us of a police car making its way rapidly toward us. Sensing my consternation, the head trader assured me that we would not have any trouble, as he paid this police officer a modest bribe every week, so that the officer would not interfere with the traders' business. Perhaps the policeman had finally decided that the bribe he received was not adequate for him to keep a blind eye any longer. Our deal was already completed by the time the police car sped onto the scene, so I was able to part at once from their company. Once safely in my upper-level hotel room, I observed from my upper-level window down to the street below an official state vehicle arrive in front of the hotel. I could see the two young men with whom I had made the black market trade being escorted into the hotel for questioning by the government official who arrived in this car. Quickly leaving my room and heading downstairs, I dashed through the lobby, and outside the hotel I jumped into an awaiting taxi to join my tour group of American teens as we headed for an evening out to a discotheque.

To me it seemed that the general regard toward Americans was positive in Russia in the early 1990s. When a Russian would ask me where I was from, when I told the Russian I was an American, I would imagine the sound of the thud of a red carpet being rolled out in front of me – that was the expectation conditioned in me from routine displays of reverence from Russians to my declaration of my nationality. Such high regard, though, was not absolute. On a beautiful, warm, sunny day in Kurgan, Russia in 1993, I started out from my host family's apartment for a walk by myself. I was startled early into my walk, when a beer bottle hurled from a high distance struck the pavement right next to me. My eyes darted upward toward a high apartment building some distance away, to a window about twelve stories up. Two drunken young males were leaning out of that window, and one of them yelled to me, "Yankee, go home!" (Americans, it seems, were easy to identify in Kurgan; a Russian friend spotted my two American colleagues in a crowd of people from a considerable distance once when we were looking for them.) I made quick, relative assessments of distances – the window from which the bottle was thrown to its impact point, and then the impact point relative to my near position; this led me to feel quite sure that the bottle was intended to strike me. I immediately returned to the safety of my host family.

Another walk I took in Kurgan, this time with a Russian friend, proved to be even more frightening. My friend and I were casually walking along the sidewalk when suddenly our way was blocked by a police jeep that turned directly in front of us and stopped across the sidewalk. My friend and I were instructed by the police to get into the back of the jeep. At first, I was not too concerned, having had no prior direct experience with the Russian police. But when my friend asked me in English in the back of the jeep if I was scared, and then he shared with me that he was scared, I became more concerned. The police claimed, falsely, that we were robbery suspects. The police drove us away from the central part of the city, and we were terrified to consider what may lie in store for us. We rode on, and as the police heard my English and slowly came to realize that I was an American, the police then subtly communicated non-verbally to one another that my friend and I should be released. The only draw of an American to this city was the well-established sister city exchange program between Kurgan and the American city counterpart in which the university at which I studied was located. The sister city exchange program was well known in Kurgan. So the police decided in their silent communication amongst themselves that beating an American participant of the sister city exchange program would be a bad course of action, so they pulled over to release us, making up the excuse that neither of the robbery suspects whom they sought wore glasses (I wore glasses). The police stopped the jeep and allowed us to get out of the vehicle. My friend and I were animated by the adrenaline rush from this experience for some time. A Russian student from our university was not as fortunate as my friend and I were, the time this other student had a run-in with the Russian police sometime earlier. This student showed me a photo taken of him in a hospital bed: his face was black and blue; the police had beaten him for no good reason, just because this student happened to be at the discotheque the police raided (probably also for no good reason). The practice of the Russian police detaining citizens under contrived accusations is known to occur not infrequently.

Another danger associated with walking about in Kurgan that I experienced related to the cold weather. On a Saturday night in the third week of November, some students from the university where I also studied wanted to meet with me. Kurgan is situated on the southern edge of the West Siberian Plain, and at that time of year it is very cold. I left the warm comfort of my host family's apartment reluctantly, wondering why I agreed to meet those students at 10:30 p.m. It was a long bus ride from near my host family's apartment to near the front gates of the university, where we agreed to meet. On the bus en route, I sat near the doors, so that I would be able to identify the stops when the doors opened along the bus route; this bus route was familiar to me, as it was the one I took when commuting to and from the university for my studies on weekdays. All the side bus windows were coated with frost from the cold outside, and the only way for me to see out of the bus was by peering out of the bus doors when they were opened at a stop. I arrived at the meeting spot a little early, and nobody was there yet, which was a relief to me, because I had decided that if no one was there yet, I would return to my host family's apartment without having to make excuses to anyone about why I didn't want to spend time with them that night. I didn't want to be rude in backing out, it's just that I had a feeling that it was better for me just to return to my host family, so I went with my feeling. So, I boarded my bus for a return trip to my host family's apartment. I sat right near the bus doors on my return trip as well, so that I could watch the stops each time the bus stopped and I could follow where we were along the route. The side windows on this bus were also covered in frost. For a number of stops, I was able to recognize landmarks. But after a while, I stopped recognizing any landmarks at bus stops when the doors would open, but I stayed on board, hoping that eventually I would see a place I recognized. Some passengers were starting to look at me with concern, as if they sensed that I'd passed my stop; I stood out as a shy, awkward foreigner from an affluent, Western nation, and as the U.S.-Russia sister-city exchange program was the only real draw of someone with my profile to this place, a quick conclusion the average citizen aboard the bus could draw was that I was one of the two or three Americans who participated each year in this well-known exchange program. No American participating in this program would be housed so far out in the outskirts of town, it could be assumed, as the goal was to make the exchange student's experience pleasant; housing located not far from the heart of the city made the exchange student feel more connected to the main action of the place, and the proximity near the university, where English-speaking students could be found without much effort, offset the severe linguistic handicap of the American exchange student who without exception struggled with a low level of proficiency in the Russian language. The interior bus lights came on, the bus came to a complete stop, and all remaining passengers disembarked. It was the end of the bus line, so I joined the disembarkation. We were outside of city limits on an unlit gravel road, and I wasn't exactly sure how to get back to my host family's apartment. I was too self-conscious about my limited proficiency in the Russian language to work up the nerve to ask anyone for help finding my way. I began walking along this gravel road in the direction from which buses approaching this final stop were coming. I was quite concerned, as it was dark, I didn't know exactly where I was -- somewhere outside of this foreign city in Russia -- and it was quite cold (cell phones were not yet in common use, so calling for help from out there to my host family – one member of which spoke English – was not an option). But to my great relief, I recognized a smokestack upon which I often gazed from my host family's kitchen window. So, I just directed myself toward that smokestack beacon and I kept walking. To my great relief, the smokestack guided me to an area with which I was familiar near my host family's apartment, so that I was able to make it the rest of the way back without further concerns.

The threat of exposure to the cold during the winter in Kurgan was a part of my daily life. There is cold, and then there is the intense cold of a Siberian winter: walking around in temperatures nearing forty degrees below zero day after day caused my exposed skin to experience a strangely combined sensation of freezing and burning. I once removed my gloves just long enough to buy eggs from a vendor on the street, and in the short time my hands were exposed to the freezing-cold air, I felt sharp pain in my fingers. The first breath I would draw upon exiting the apartment building where I lived, as I began my hour-long walk to the university, was always a shock to my system. One day, a Russian friend and I were walking toward his home after a rehearsal for his band, with which I had rehearsed as a guest singer, and everything seemed fine, walking outside in the cold, until suddenly my friend (the same one with whom I was put in the back of the police jeep) looked alarmed, and he told me that we needed to get inside the nearest building quickly. The tip of my nose was white, a sign that frostbite would set in soon. Safely inside an electronics store, my friend instructed me to cup my hands around my nose and to inhale and exhale repeatedly in order to warm my nose up. I did this for a while, we waited inside the store for several minutes so that my nose could warm up, and then we headed back onto the street. I am grateful that this friend noticed that the tip of my nose was white, since I felt no pain or discomfort whatsoever on my nose.

But the cold was not the most serious environmental hazard in Kurgan. The Schuch'ye Chemical Weapons Destruction Facility, located 110 miles from Kurgan, Russia, was constructed in near proximity to a massive stockpile of Russia's chemical weapons, including nerve gas, which were stored in the Kurgan region; the location of Schuch'ye made transportation of these stored chemical weapons to Schuch'ye for destruction convenient, as the distance between the stockpiles and Schuch'ye was not far. I had lived in and left Kurgan prior to the construction of Schuch'ye and the subsequent destruction of these chemical weapons stored in the Kurgan region, so who knows what I was exposed to. What I had observed of the generally loose regard toward the handling of pollutants in Russia gave me reason to believe that the storage facilities for these chemical weapons were likely sloppy outfits. One day while I was walking somewhere through a bustling area of Kurgan, I came upon a large pool of a green liquid filling a dirt hole in the ground; the substance reminded me of green Windex, or something synthetic like antifreeze, and there was a large pool of it, filling a dirt hole that had been dug there, with no barricades to prevent anyone from falling into it. Within a day or two, the ground was covered over, and the pool of the green substance was gone. Where had it gone? A few days later, a pool of the same toxic-looking, green substance was there again, in the very same spot.

The area with the most radioactive contamination on planet Earth is located in the Chelyabinsk Province, with its capital city Chelyabinsk located three-and-a-half hours by bus from Kurgan. I observed, from a bus window while entering the Chelyabinsk city limits, factories situated along a lakeshore, one right next to the other, like stacks of children's building blocks; this view was my snapshot of the massive scale of heavily polluting industry in Chelyabinsk. The Mayak nuclear reactor, located in the Chelyabinsk region, produced plutonium for nuclear weapons; this facility dumped untreated nuclear waste directly into the local river for decades, where locals, oblivious to the contamination of the river (since the Soviet government kept the dumping of untreated nuclear waste a secret from the populace) would fish. In 1957, an accident occurred at Mayak that released an amount of radiation exceeded only by that of the Chernobyl meltdown in 1986. The level of radioactivity in the Chelyabinsk region remains alarmingly high to this day, and cancer rates are well above average.

The Kurgan and Chelyabinsk regions comprise an area of massive environmental contamination. When I returned from having spent 10 consecutive months in Kurgan (I spent an additional four months there a few years prior), I experienced for a while these strange mental episodes when I would wake up from a nap, and my mind would be a blank slate. I was aware of the enclosure of walls, but I would just need to get outside to clear my head. These episodes eventually went away, but I'll always wonder if they were caused by something I was exposed to while living in Kurgan. Years later, I challenged the American university program coordinator for the exchange program to Kurgan regarding the safety of sending American students to Kurgan; this program coordinator assured me that a consultation on the safety of sending students to Kurgan had been made with one of his colleagues, a professor of science at the university, before it was decided to allow students to study in Kurgan. Although this professor of science argued that it was safe to send students there, it feels to me as though we American exchange-program participants to Kurgan were subject to very real risks to our health, all in the name of a sister-city exchange program, study abroad, and multiculturalism.

Within a few short years following the collapse of the Soviet Union, the hopes many Russians had held in the late 1980s and early 1990s of Russia developing a system of freedom and prosperity, such as was enjoyed in the United States, had faded. Also, that favorable regard of Russians toward Americans had declined and melded with widespread xenophobia. One time when I was aboard a train in Russia, a woman was going cabin to cabin selling her handmade, white, lacy shawls. The woman tried to sell me a shawl, and once she realized that I wasn't Russian, she became much more aggressive in her sales approach. The Russians with whom I was sharing this cabin – all strangers to me – urged the woman to leave me alone, but she defended herself, exclaiming, "He's not ours! He's not ours!" -- meaning he's not Russian, so this in her mind was justification enough to her to apply more pressure to me in an attempt to get me to buy one of her shawls. Such an attitude toward foreigners, regardless of the attitudes of the individual passengers in my train cabin, was commonplace enough to have legs to stand on in a public space in Russia. In the late 1990s, foreigners in Russia were required to pay double the price for hotels, planes, and trains. During my time as a visiting scholar at Moscow State University, I had difficulty connecting with Russian students, and the general regard to non-Russians by Russians, as I saw it, was one of unfriendliness. (It was the Chinese students living on my dormitory floor with whom I formed friendly bonds.) Once at a Moscow Metro ticket counter during the time I was studying at Moscow State University, I asked a ticket agent a question and she told me she would call the police on me, for no valid reason that I could see -- I had asked her a perfectly reasonable question. I guess my offense was that I was a foreigner. On one occasion a number of years earlier, I asked a Metro worker for directions, and she immediately asked where I was from, to which I replied in Russian, "What does it matter?" Aghast, she twice repeated my question, mockingly: "What does it matter?!?" -- as if she couldn't imagine a question that would matter more. In Kurgan, I would be walking down the street, and when encountering a couple of Russians walking together, I would hear one of them remark to the other, in regards to me, *Inostranets*, which means "foreigner." The occurrence of being outed publicly as a foreigner in this way was so shocking and frequent, that I almost supposed its occurrence was just in my head. Naturally, I felt very self-conscious about being a foreigner in Russia. The level of complete ignorance toward different nationalities can be extreme among some Russians. I had a teacher in Moscow who told me about a young African man he knew who went to a *banya* (bathing house) in Moscow, and the African was asked by a Russian who was there if the brown color from his skin would wash off.

A foreigner in Russia always feels like an outsider, which can make him particularly vulnerable to the police, but the degree of targeting by the police varies based on the ethnicity of the foreigner. A teacher in Moscow offered my class of Americans general tips on how to avoid problems with the police -- tips useful for Russians also, but especially valuable for us Americans in helping us dismantle some of our problem-inviting naivete. The teacher's tips for us were the following: don't make eye contact with the Russian police, as the police consider eye contact to be an act of confrontation; also, carry a newspaper in order to appear educated, as the police are less likely to target educated people. When it comes to being a foreigner in Russia though, a person is better off being white, and the whiter the better; this attitude is embraced by public safety officers, i.e., the police and security guards: racial profiling by the police was legal in Russia at that time. Once I was walking in the Moscow Underground, when directly in front of me, a harmless-looking Asian mother and her young adult daughter were randomly stopped by a policeman for no apparent reason, and the women were asked to show their documents; the women appeared quite harmless, and they should have drawn less attention from the police than I should have, I thought, as I was dressed in purple dragon pants, had tattoos visible on my forearms, and also wore earrings. As I would enter the first of a double layer of security to get into the dormitory where I lived at Moscow State University, I would watch as the security guards would subject the Asian students to more rigorous screening; the security guards would ask them, "Don't you have any other documents?" -- their student identifications not being considered sufficient by the security guards. I would approach the security guards, show my student identification, they would look at it, then look at me with my Nordic features as if to say,

"Why are you still standing here?" I was on my way through without ever being asked for a second piece of identification.

One time while walking underground toward a Metro subway train in Moscow, I came upon a large group of young men who were chanting vociferously. Walking past the group, I did not feel threatened by them, but I also did not understand what they were chanting about. I boarded a subway train, and many members of this group of men entered the same car as I had entered, and they resumed their chants very loudly for all the passengers on the crowded subway car to hear. I understood that their chants were about something horrible, judging by how much alarm, disgust, and shock a woman seated near me showed in reaction to what she heard from them. I also sensed this woman pleading with me through body language not to dare do anything that would reveal me to be a foreigner to the chanting men. As a foreigner, I paid keen attention to the perception of non-verbal signals, such as those from the woman seated near me, as a way to compensate for my limitations with the Russian language when it came to making sense of such puzzling banter. I am of Scandinavian descent, which helped me blend in to some degree in Russia; this may have been my saving grace on this subway ride. The Swedish student who was my next-door neighbor in our dormitory told me later that day that the day marked Adolf Hitler's birthday; this Swedish student had seen neo-Nazis out earlier in the day, so it then became obvious to me that these men who were chanting and shocking subway passengers with their words were celebrating the birth of Adolf Hitler and glorifying Nazism. (This Swedish student often bragged about never being stopped by the police to show his documents – police randomly asking people to show their documents is a common practice in Russia – and he plausibly attributed this good luck with the police to his ethnicity.) So, while xenophobia is endemic in Russia, there are greater or lesser degrees of tolerance of foreigners by Russians on the basis of their ethnicity.

I appeared Russian enough the time I visited a Russian prison. I have tattoos on my forearms, and a man presumed to be Russian who has tattoos is likely to encounter problems in Russia, and indeed, my tattoos were an issue at this prison. I was one of an American group of students visiting Vladimir Central Prison, formerly a political prison, the former inmates of which included the American spy Gary Powers and Vasily Iosifovich Stalin, son of Joseph Stalin. As we Americans were concluding our tour of the prison, some prison guards took me aside in the prison yard and carefully examined my passport. My tattoos had drawn the suspicion of the guards. In Russia, tattoos typically indicate that the wearer either has a history of military service, a prison record, or is a member of a gang. The guards wanted to make sure that I wasn't a prisoner being smuggled out by this tour group. (A Russian citizen once told me in Russia that Russians might be leerier of me as a foreigner with my tattoos than they would be of other Russians with tattoos; the meanings of tattoos worn by Russians would be familiar to the average Russian, so the average Russian would be better prepared for how to deal with a Russian man with tattoos, whereas with me and my unfamiliar tattoos, I could be considered to be a greater threat, as Russians wouldn't know what my tattoos represented.) This screening by the prison guards to determine if I was a prisoner being smuggled out, which rattled me, followed an incident earlier during our prison tour, when I took one errant step away from our group, thus one step closer to the unrestrained prisoners in the yard; this prompted our tour guide to snatch me back into line with our group. Our tour guide told us later that the prisoners could have tried to take one of us Americans hostage, and they then would have good leverage to make their demands in exchange for the release of an American hostage. The host family father with whom I lived in Vladimir was a prison guard at Vladimir Central Prison, and he talked about how the roles blurred between guards and convicts due to the two groups being in such close proximity day after day. Our tour group walked through the prison yard, where the prisoners stood freely to the side, those prisoners making strange calls and comments; the place had the feel of an open zoo for dangerous animals, and it wasn't obvious which group, guards or prisoners, was in charge of the place.

It's not easy being a foreigner in Russia. Being outed as a foreigner creates a psychological strain on the foreigner. The naïve foreigner at first is likely unaware of the lingering and revived manifestations of totalitarianism in Russian society. A naïve foreigner from a freer and more democratic country would be expected to be shocked by the disregard for more democratic assumptions of privacy that defines Russian, post-Soviet totalitarianism. One time when I was a passenger on a ship cruise of the Volga waterways, I met a young Russian woman who was working as a receptionist on the cruise ship. She and I became interested in one another, as two bodies of opposite sexes sometimes do. We would talk casually while she worked at her desk, and her manner would be relaxed and pleasant, but there were occasions when a certain strange man would sit or stand nearby and watch us, and this receptionist would become tense and more reluctant to converse with me under the stranger's eye. Let's suppose, for lack of a better explanation, that this man was a Russian intelligence officer (and my acquaintance likely knew he was, which is why she acted around him the way she did; I later wrote to this former receptionist and asked her who that man was, but she never responded). Under xenophobic, privacy-restricted Russian autocracy, a cruise ship populated by a hundred young American passengers would be a bounty for intelligence gathering; hence the presence of intelligence operatives onboard to surveil the many conversations amongst the Americans and their Russian student mentors. On one occasion when I was out to dinner in Moscow with a couple of fellow Moscow State University students from China, two men were at a nearby table watching us and listening to us. The men had serious looks on their faces, as if it were their jobs to observe us in some official capacity. My feelers for suspicious characters are finely tuned, so these presumed intelligence agents had drawn my attention early during our dinner. I decided to have a little fun with them: my proficiency in the Russian language was quite good by this point, better than that of my Chinese dinner companions, so I took on the role of spokesperson for my table, using the Russian language, for the audience of the men presumably surveilling us. The day marked a Soviet holiday, and I found it outrageous that Russians would still celebrate Soviet holidays. To my audience of the two presumed intelligence agents, I shared my pocket political view of the Soviet government: "They butchered the language, the religion, the people – Enjoy the holiday!"

The average Russian might be disciplined by the authorities for making such a statement, but as a foreigner who could speak Russian, I was more insulated – it probably wouldn't be that way now in 2025; this was 2008. Perhaps the men were just grumpy and disliked foreigners, but once I became aware of being surveilled in Russia, I was primed to look for it, so that if I was just being paranoid on this occasion, it was justified paranoia.

Xenophobia – the fear of foreigners – is widespread in Russia. In the 1990s, foreigners were required to provide a negative test result for HIV before being admitted into Russia, the subtext to this requirement being that foreigners bringing HIV and AIDS into Russia were responsible for the AIDS epidemic in Russia. This was absurd, since Russia had a very serious, internally-produced problem with HIV and AIDS. But as regards serious illnesses in Russia, alcoholism is the most widespread disease. I didn't want this disease to infect me, which is why I quit drinking alcohol in Russia. Leading up to my decision to quit drinking alcohol, the university rector in Kurgan once invited me into his office for a drink and proceeded to pour me a full glass of vodka – not a shot, but a glass – which I drank, as a show of respect to the rector's office and a show of disrespect to my body. Russian men tend to be much heavier drinkers than Russian women. The men inflict tremendous pressure on women and reluctant men to consume large amounts of alcohol at dinner parties: a simple refusal to drink is not left unchallenged. Those Russian women whom I observed at dinner and drinking parties found ways to resist the insistence of the male guests to drink excessively: these Russian women would nurse glasses of champagne to defend against the male guests' insistence on more excessive drinking. But male holdouts against excessive drinking have their defenses knocked away from all sides: "Drink! Drink! Eat! Eat!" I had to display an absolutism in my refusal to drink alcohol in Russia, in order not to develop the type of serious drinking problem so commonplace there.

A common sight in Kurgan was of men staggering drunk, covered from head to toe in mud after they'd fallen down into mud puddles. Sometimes, an embarrassed wife would be escorting a dazed-eyed passenger on rough seas home from a party. Men passed out drunk in snowbanks by the side of the road was something I witnessed a few times. I never saw any drivers stopping to help to prevent these passed out men from freezing to death.

There is a pattern of destructive behavior among Russian men: with alcohol toward themselves and their families, with violence also against themselves and others. I saw plenty of instances during the time I spent in Russia in the 1990s. One time I decided to wait overnight at a major train station in Moscow for my departure the following day, rather than to spend the night in a hotel. Part of my reason for this decision to wait overnight in the train station was because I was too shy to go to a hotel to get a room for myself, and part of it was just for the adventure. The area just outside the terminal -- a large, open platform -- looked like a safe-enough place in the late afternoon, as there were multitudes of people awaiting their departures. As the late afternoon turned to evening, fewer and fewer people remained in this area, and I began to feel uneasy when I lost the safety of the crowd. Then when two policemen wearing bulletproof vests and carrying assault rifles entered the square for their patrol, I understood that the place where I was to spend the night was not exactly safe. Arbatskaya Railway Station, Moscow: The World's Most Dangerous Zoo.

As darkness settled and very few people remained in this outside area, I went inside the train station in order to find a safe place to remain until dawn; I just had to make it until 5:30 a.m. when the subway opened. By about 10:45 p.m., there were hardly any people around in this enormous train station. There was one woman with a small stand selling hot drinks, she and her stand dwarfed in size by the vast space and sky-high ceilings in the massive hall; otherwise this area of the station was mostly empty. My plan was to remain near this woman throughout the night for safety. Not long after staking my space near the hot drinks lady, a deranged, bare-chested man smashed his fists right through the glass on some entrance doors to the train station, which were located a short distance from where I was standing. Entering the hall, this bare-chested maniac grabbed a woman, put a knife to her throat, then dragged the screaming woman up a long flight of stairs. Upstairs there was more breaking glass and screaming, and people were running out of that upstairs waiting area. At the base of the stairs, where the woman had been snatched at knifepoint, there were several, young, frightened policemen helplessly standing around, trying to decide how to confront this maniac. Eventually the violent episode ended when the man was apprehended. He was taken into a room on the ground floor, presumably for interrogation, not far from where I was bracing myself. After some time had passed with the dangerous man being questioned in the room, I had a horrible fright when I saw the police walking with the perpetrator in my direction, but this highly dangerous man was walking freely, not in handcuffs, as the police followed him a few paces behind. The criminal walked right past me, and I wondered if I would be his next hostage. Fortunately, he walked past me as the police followed behind him.

Another incident at a train station in Moscow to which I was a witness proved to be even more dangerous. My two American classmates and I, while traveling aboard a train in Russia, became acquainted with a congenial man, who, as were we, was traveling from Kurgan to Moscow. This man offered to help my American classmates and me get a taxi cab once we arrived in Moscow; the three of us gladly accepted his offer. This pleasant man was an ethnic minority of dark complexion; it may have been that he was from a Soviet breakaway republic, as tensions felt by Russians against citizens from Soviet breakaway republics were high at this time – this geopolitical strife may have been what led to the situation that unfolded a short time later. The man appeared Central Asian to me. This Central Asian man stood with me and my classmates next to a major thoroughfare consisting of numerous traffic lanes, though now quite quiet, as it was four in the morning. Suddenly, two Russian men in black leather jackets and black pants approached us on the sidewalk, and right away the three men -- the two Russian men in black against our new Central Asian acquaintance – began to argue. The three men stood there arguing in English, strangely enough, and as I happened to lower my view toward the men, I saw to my alarm that one of the men in black was holding a pistol, pointing the gun directly toward the abdomen of our kind new acquaintance. I very carefully started to move away – we were all standing within a few feet of each other, and it was unsafe for me to inform my American classmates that a gun was being pointed at our new acquaintance, so I hoped my classmates would notice the gun on their own and do their best to find safety. The streets were wide open, there not being much in the vicinity to hide behind, neither trees, nor cars, nor buildings; there was mostly just flat cement in all directions with little cover. After arguing for a while, the two men in black leather walked away, and I felt relieved that the situation hadn't escalated further. When the two men in black were down the sidewalk a short distance, our new acquaintance stupidly shouted something at them. Enraged, the man with the gun turned, pointed the gun sideways straight at our acquaintance's head, shouting and marching straight toward him. I was sure the aggressor was going to blow our acquaintance's head off. Somehow, the trigger wasn't pulled, they argued briefly some more, then the men in black turned and marched off. This new acquaintance of ours, who nearly had his head blown off a moment before, took on a nonchalant air, as if this sort of thing happened all the time. A taxi cab arrived to drive my American classmates and me away from the scene, as we rode along, feeling stunned.

The piece of advice I would most readily give to anyone making a trip to Russia would be that he or she should exercise extreme caution while crossing a street, and should never jaywalk or cross an intersection on a red light, no matter how many people were doing it. One day in Kurgan, while walking to the fitness center after my day of teaching at the university, I noticed a few people milling around on the opposite side of the street in a way that caused me to pause. Understanding that the matter for attention was in the street, I looked into the street to see a woman in her late sixties lying dead there; she had been struck by a car while crossing the street outside of a pedestrian crosswalk. She had one arm extended out past her head still clutching her purse, one of her black boots was off in the street, and her brains were squished on the pavement. On another occasion, our group of American students studying Russian in Vladimir for the summer had just returned from a weekend trip to a nearby city, and we were all waiting at a tram stop, so that each of us may return to his or her host family's apartment. One of my classmates directed my attention to a female teenager; this classmate seemed amused with her, the reason for which wasn't clear to me, but the significance of this detail is that he had drawn my attention to her, whereas before I hadn't noticed her. Within a few moments, an automobile came racing through a red light and struck this teenage girl as she walked through the crosswalk. I heard the impact, and either I looked away, or I happened to be looking at a shop window behind me when it happened, but I saw reflected in that store window the body of the girl flying up into the air, and her body looked broken. The driver who struck her came rushing out of the car, in a panic running toward a store to call an ambulance, and in his state of alarm, he asked our American guide, "She walked right out in front of me, didn't she?!?" to which our guide replied, "It doesn't matter, you had a red light." The girl lay in the street with a trickle of urine running from her body. The driver's young male friend got out of the passenger side of the automobile to look at the place of impact on the automobile to assess the damage done to the vehicle. Yes, the driver's friend was concerned with the damage done to the car while the victim of his friend's aggressive driving lay dying in the street. The paramedics arrived, put her in the back of the ambulance, but the ambulance did not drive off immediately, which was a bad sign. We later found out from one of our teachers who inquired at our request that the girl in fact had died. What was also troubling about this matter was the indifferent reaction I got from the Russians to whom I reported this fatal collision. Indifference to trauma seems to be a part of the Russian psyche, or such indifferent regards are a manifestation of the cultural normalization response to the disturbing; too many things in Russia are disturbing to be bothered by all of them.

Yet perhaps it could be that this indifference to a person's death is typical when the deceased person is unknown, but in cases when the deceased is known, more concern and sympathy tend to be felt and expressed. One day, as I was exiting an apartment building where I lived with one host family in Kurgan, I reached the bottom of the stairs at the street level to find that a bunch of beautiful, red carnations had been dropped all over in front of the apartment building. The carnations were in perfect condition, and I thought, what a waste for these red carnations not to be enjoyed, rather than just lying there in the dirty snow! So, I decided to gather the red carnations and take them back up to my host family's apartment; my host family was gone, and I wanted to surprise them when they returned, so I arranged a bouquet of the red carnations in a small vase and placed the bouquet on the kitchen table. I then started out again for my original destination before I was sidetracked: the library. Back at my host family's apartment after spending some time at the library, I discovered that the bouquet of red carnations I had arranged was gone. "How rude!" I thought. I couldn't understand why my host family would throw out the bouquet. But a member of my host family explained to me that someone in our apartment building had died, and in Russia, it is a custom that when a close acquaintance or family member dies, red carnations are scattered before the door of the deceased.

What makes travel exotic is the unfamiliarity of the place and the people. I and my American classmates from the Kurgan program took a week-long holiday to Mineralnye Vody, Russia, a city located just north of the Caucasus Mountains. This place seemed quite exotic to us. Our hosts in Mineralnye Vody, a husband and wife, were both doctors. One afternoon, these hosts informed us three Americans that we had been invited to dine with another married couple with whom our doctor hosts were friends. The male dinner host, the husband, arrived to take us to his home in his automobile, so we stepped outside into the heavy snow to make his acquaintance, and to go with him. To our surprise, there stood an American Lincoln stretch limousine, the host's personal vehicle, waiting to transport us the three or four short blocks to this host's home. Our host, who was Armenian, stood by his limousine with a beaming smile, proud to flaunt this display of his wealth. Our male doctor host, with whom we stayed in Mineralnye Vody for the week, became acquainted with the Armenian man, the dinner host, after the doctor cared for the Armenian man's wife -- also Armenian – when she was hospitalized with a broken arm after her husband threw her out of a second-story window of their home. This victim of marital defenestration is the one who served us dinner that evening. It was said in the 1990s that the only way to get rich in Russia was by unlawful means.

Our doctor hosts took me and my American classmates to the train station in Mineralnye Vody when it was time for us to return to Kurgan. At the train station, our hosts bought us a few light provisions for our 63-hour train ride. The provisions consisted of hard-boiled eggs, bread, and cheese. We weren't provided with much or anything to drink by our hosts. We knew of no restaurant car on the train, where we could have purchased drinks (I personally never noticed a restaurant car on a train during the numerous times I traveled by train in Russia). My classmates and I had taken the 36-hour train ride between Moscow and Kurgan before, which is when we learned that items to eat and drink could be purchased at train stops along the way: villagers come running up to the trains to sell baskets of fruits (especially apples), and drinks. Again, the duration of the journey from Mineralnye Vody to Kurgan was 63 hours, so it was much further than the 36-hour Moscow-Kurgan train route with which we were familiar. Every stop along the route between Mineralnye Vody and Kurgan drew villagers selling items such as scarves and vases, but no one was selling anything to drink, nor any produce. The more places we stopped without there being drinks or produce sold, the more concerned we became about our thirst. When we stopped at one prominent train station in a large city about three-quarters of the way through our trip, I rushed off the train, purchased at a kiosk a carton of orange juice, then I jumped back onto the train with little time to spare before the train departed again. Being left by the train was a reasonable concern, considering our unfamiliarity with the train timetable. When I jumped off the train, I had to guess from the behavior of other passengers hopping off our train how much time we likely had to get back on board. Throngs of people were bustling about, and there was no conductor checking that everyone reboarded. We three naïve travelers consumed the carton of juice amongst ourselves in short order -- it wasn't nearly enough fluid to rehydrate us. Upon reaching my host family's apartment in Kurgan, I was so thirsty that I drank 13 cups of tea (drinking water straight from the tap isn't safe), one after another, in order to rehydrate myself after that 63-hour train journey during which we had little to drink. On some later train trip in Russia, I finally noticed, to my embarrassment, a hot water tap at the end of the car I was in: every car on a Russian passenger train has a hot water tap to be used for making tea.

Usually -- our train trip between Mineralnye Vody and Kurgan being an exception – it is quite common for villagers to meet the trains with drinks and food for sale, along the many stops that trains make throughout the Russian countryside. It's a short window of time when these villagers can make their sales before the trains leave for the next stop. In these remote areas, the sale of produce to train passengers represents an important source of income for these villagers, who are surrounded by vast stretches of countryside and as such are isolated in their microeconomies. So, these villagers must capitalize on opportunities to sell their produce when infrequent trains make brief stops near their villages. I once witnessed a male train passenger haggling with a female villager over the price he would pay her for her bucket of apples. This passenger was reluctant to pay an amount that seemed fair to the villager. The villager was clearly getting impatient, as she looked ahead toward the front of the train, knowing that the train would depart soon; being buttonholed by this man was costing her precious time that she could be using to make more quick sales. With only moments remaining before the train was to depart, with no time left for this villager to make any more sales, the male passenger finally agreed to a price for the bucket of apples, and then he reached his hand into his pocket and withdrew an enormous wad of Russian rubles. The passenger had made a power play of the obscene amount of cash he had on his person at the expense of this poor villager, who was trying to earn from the sale of her bucket of apples a sliver of the amount of money this man had in his pocket.

Each time a train or bus I would be on in Russia would stop, it would always be a gamble for me to make it back on board in time before the train or bus would depart anew; although timetables are posted prevalently on trains, the information never seemed very reliable to me. The problem was greater on buses, since timetables are not posted in the areas of passenger seating. On my trip from Mineralnye Vody to Kurgan, I succeeded in dashing on and off the train in time during its brief stop to purchase a box of orange juice, but on another occasion when traveling by public transportation in Russia, I was not so fortunate. On this other occasion, traveling between Tyumen' and Kurgan by bus, the amount of time the bus stopped was shorter than I expected, and I was distracted anyway by some snack food items that had caught my eye, on display behind the glass, front viewing window of one kiosk. On a previous trip between these two cities, I had gotten off at this same stop, and on that occasion it seemed as though the bus remained at the stop for a longer period of time, which was why during this second time stopping here I didn't feel rushed. The distance between Tyumen' and Kurgan, Siberia, is 130 miles, and here I was between the two cities at a stop with few amenities, a lonely spot interrupting stretches of countryside. A hole dug in the ground served as the public toilet, and around it for privacy within arm's reach were four short walls made from wooden slats. The feeling of privacy within this primitive toilet was incomplete, as the open sky above stared down. I was leisurely window shopping at the food items for sale at the kiosk, when my attention was grabbed by the sound of my bus starting down the road without me in it. I chased after the bus, and fortunately, a passenger must have seen me running behind the bus and alerted the driver, for the bus then pulled to the side of the road. The bus was already down the road far enough for me to have to continue running for a while in order to catch up to it once it had stopped. Out of breath as I entered the bus, I thanked the driver for stopping for me: *Sbasibo!* I couldn't have called anyone conveniently, as cell phones were not then in common use. I likely had no telephone numbers for contacts in Kurgan on my person; I could only have provided to somebody I may have asked for help the full name of one university teacher from my program in Kurgan. I'm sure I could have figured a way out of being stranded at this place -- the rule in such situations is to find someone young who looks educated and use English to ask for help (though this may have been more difficult this far removed from a significant population center where the general level of education would be higher). Years later, once my knowledge of the Russian language became better, this situation would not have been nearly so frightening, but at the time of my life when this episode of nearly being stranded occurred, my low level of proficiency in the Russian language, my high degree of shyness, and my still limited travel experience all made the scenario in which I would have needed to seek help getting back to Kurgan one that I'm glad I wasn't required to confront.

I fumbled often in my attempts to use the Russian language early in my studies. It was certainly more amusing for me to witness Russians fumbling with their use of the English language. The product I peddled as an English language teacher was the American dialect of English. Many Russians were enamored with American culture in the 1990s. There was a poster hanging inside one of the Kurgan public buses I rode on of an attractive, young blonde woman wearing a bikini and holding an assault rifle, and the caption at the bottom of the poster read "Don't Mess with the U.S.A."; the poster image was in such juxtaposition to the atmosphere on the bus, with all the passengers bundled in heavy, dark, coarse clothing, all looking rather ground down by life aboard the rickety, Soviet-era, yellow, Hungarian bus, the atmosphere made even dingier by the muddy snow the bus and passengers all had to make their way through. Against such a backdrop of a bizarre preoccupation with American culture (similar examples were to be found all around), one American student in Kurgan had enthusiastic support at the university for her staging of what she considered to be an American-style celebration of Halloween. To me though, the Halloween party this American student organized more closely resembled a typical Russian party, as this Halloween party, like a typical Russian party, featured many dishes of food laid out on long tables; the only Halloween-themed addition to the party was a game of bobbing for apples. This American Halloween party organizer and I, the only two Americans teaching at the university that year, were asked by a local Russian television reporter who was covering this "American" Halloween party, "Is this how you celebrate Halloween in the US?" My compatriot answered affirmatively, that this is how Halloween is celebrated in the U.S. (her response was not surprising, since she was the organizer of the party). Then the television reporter asked me the same question, if this is how Halloween is celebrated in the U.S., and I replied that no, this is not how Halloween is celebrated in the U.S.; then I went on to explain how children in the U.S. go treat-or-treating on Halloween. For the broadcast of this news report on television, our two interviews were shown back-to-back; One American viewpoint: Yes, this is how Halloween is celebrated in America; Another American viewpoint: No, this is not how Halloween is celebrated in America. The contrast between our responses was amusing, but what was most amusing about the broadcast had to do with how my American colleague concluded her description of the American Halloween celebration by using the idiomatic expression "That's it in a nutshell"; this idiomatic expression was unfamiliar to whomever was tasked with interpreting the interview from English into Russian, so the interpreter took an unfigurative understanding of the "nutshell" remark: the Russian interpretation came out as (if one were to interpret the remark back into English) "That's how they do it in Nutshell," as if Nutshell were a community in America, and the American teacher's description of the celebration of Halloween related to how it is done in Nutshell, U.S.A.

At the heart of any typical Russian celebration is food. A typical party as I experienced in the company of young Russian adults involved everybody being seated at a table set with many delicious dishes of food. Eating, drinking, and conversing at these parties go on for quite some time, and it is not out of the ordinary for the table to be pushed to the wall following dinner, so that dancing may commence. Some guests remain at or return to the table for talking and nibbling, while others dance. Dining and drinking remain the main activities for the duration of a Russian party, and a Russian party goes on for hours.

Most dishes of food served at Russian dinner parties are colorful and palatable, but there were some aspects of Russian food culture as I experienced them that were unappealing. One day in Kurgan, while I was walking home from the market, I saw a woman who was walking in front of me carrying a large boar's head in a burlap bag, and blood was leaking through the bag to the pavement below. Seeing this, my mind semi-automatically conjured the Russian great equalizing expression "That's normal," although, on the contrary, the sight was something that, relative to my general life experiences heretofore, I should have considered completely unusual. We don't eat animal brains in my country, and we don't carry large animal heads in burlap bags home from an unsanitary food market (the market was inside a Quonset). I can still hear the satisfied slurping noise a host in Kurgan made when she sucked the eyeballs out of the fish on her plate. One evening, the same host served me a soup that tasted like a hot nosebleed. There was a small piece of bone floating in the soup. Was this animal placenta? I never learned. But walking to the university the next day, I thought that this was just another exotic experience from my time in Russia to share with people back home. My feeling changed at dinner that night when again, I was served another piping hot dish of nosebleed soup.

Russians tend to be incredibly gracious hosts. This trait is so commonplace, that it is easy to assume that all hosts in Russia behave in this manner. I assumed such graciousness with one particular Russian woman who hosted me. I as a seasoned guest in Russian homes felt I could assume that eating food in the host home where I was living would be on standing offer, but this was not the case with this particular hostess. This hostess felt it was not her responsibility to feed me; this attitude was conveyed not by words, as there was a near-total language barrier, but by her bizarre actions. Upset that I would eat some of her garden tomatoes, she locked the door into a room where she kept her tomatoes so that I could not get to them. But the real problem this created was that where she kept her tomatoes was in the main living room of the apartment, where the telephone was located, so that if my mother called from back home, I could not get to the phone past the locked door (again, this was before cell phones were in common use). I was in a food battle with this hostess. I defied her coarse restrictions, and I helped myself to what I could find to eat when she was not around; she was terribly mean, and her meanness only made me feel more resolute about eating her food. One time, I found some chicken in the refrigerator, and I ate some of the pieces. The next day I was horrified to find my hostess in the kitchen running that chicken through a meat grinder. The chicken I had eaten was raw. The woman was unsympathetic to my panic over the possibility of getting very sick from having eaten raw chicken. Fortunately, I never got sick. The thought of possibly having to go to a Russian hospital only caused me to worry more.

But these negative experiences I had with food in Russia were more the exception. Many Russian dishes I tasted were quite delicious, and I was especially fond of the soups. Our Russian hostess in Mineralnye Vody was all business in the kitchen, working for hours on a meal, and none of us three Americans were permitted to enter the kitchen as she prepared the meals. I heartily slurped down three bowls of a delicious soup she prepared at one meal. We three Americans referred to her meals as "happy meals," as we would be filled with gaiety upon returning to our rooms from her table.

Tyumen', West Siberia, is where I had my first experience eating ice cream sold on the street during the winter. In Tyumen', as in other Russian cities, ice cream is sold on the street by women dressed in white coats that resemble the white lab coats worn by scientists, and these coats are worn by the ice cream vendors in the frigid, winter weather. It seems the long, white coats are intended to lend an air of professionalism to the ice cream vendors, and to instill confidence in the ice cream purchaser regarding the quality of the product. Strangely, it tasted great eating ice cream outside in -40 degree weather (-40 Celsius and Fahrenheit, as they are the same at this temperature); this experience was a pleasant disruption to my conditioning that something hot should be eaten in extremely cold weather. Knowing Russians, there probably exists some well-held belief that eating ice cream outside in extremely cold weather is good for the health; Russians always have such peculiar notions rooted in folklore and superstition. Eating the delicious ice cream outside in the cold weather was a profound experience: it was incredibly beautiful there in Tyumen' in December, for the hoarfrost was glistening silvery and white in the trees in the sun, and all around it felt like an enchanted winter wonderland.

The Russian landscape holds captivating beauty. The waterways of the Volga River Basin carve through some relaxing stretches of timeless greenery; I was lucky to have had the opportunities on two consecutive summers to be a passenger on two, week-long boat cruises down the Volga waterways. On the second excursion I took down the Volga -- such a cruise would be a once-in-a-lifetime experience for many Russians -- I briefly was allowed to steer the ship hosting 400 passengers. Our group of Americans was invited to visit the captain's chambers, and in there I asked if I could steer the ship. The captain assented. On this second Volga River excursion, it was also the second time I was part of a group of Americans invited into the captain's chamber, so the novelty of being invited into the captain's chamber was gone, and I felt inclined to make more out of the experience, which is why I asked the captain (not the same captain as on my first excursion) if I could steer the ship. So, I had the experience for a few moments of being at the helm of a Russian cruise ship with the lives of those hundreds of passengers in my hands; I turned the helm just slightly, with the captain's permission, in order to experience the movement of the ship under my slight navigation.

The last time I was in Russia, and certainly the final time I'll ever be there, was when I spent the spring of 2008 as a visiting scholar at Moscow State University (MGU). My advisor there invited me to attend her bi-weekly linguistics lecture class, conducted entirely in Russian for 100-150 undergraduate students. Usually during these lectures, I would only follow intermittently that, about which this professor was lecturing, but I had one moment of glory, when I was following right along with what the professor was saying. She was discussing a topic of historical Slavic linguistics in which my knowledge was strong. I was writing notes in such a flurry that it caused some of the students seated in front of me to turn their heads back to look at me. All those years of hard study, and there I was, for a moment, completely on top of the topic over and above a lecture room full of top Russian undergraduates. And then in a moment, I was lost again.

In order to swim at the Moscow State University swimming pool, I was required to pass lab screenings of my fecal and blood samples, as well as to pass a chest x-ray testing for tuberculosis; the final step of the process was to have a certificate allowing me to swim officially signed and stamped at a certain university office. When I brought to the lab for analysis my urine sample in a medical-grade specimen jar, to my astonishment I saw people bringing in their urine samples in mason jars, placing them on a rickety cart situated at the front of the waiting room, the glass jars filled with urine placed in plain sight for the many people gathered there. After I placed my urine sample on the cart along with the other samples, it was pointed out to me by a lab technician that I had misread the lab form, and that I had used my jar for a urine sample, when instead I was supposed to use the jar for a fecal sample. The lab worker who explained this to me did so by dumbing down her explanation to me-the-foreigner in Russian baby talk, saying it was poo-poo, not pee-pee, that was required in the specimen jar.

So, I brought my stool sample in a transparent specimen jar into the lab the following day. I walked into the lab to inquire as to where I should discretely place my stool sample in the transparent jar, and the lab worker gestured with her hand in one direction, and I thought she said, "There with the others," by which I thought she meant there on the cart with the jars of urine samples in the waiting room, in clear view for everyone. I thought it seemed strange to place my stool sample there, but I also thought placing urine samples – many in mason jars -- on a cart in a crowded waiting room also seemed strange, so I placed my stool sample along with the urine samples there, for all those people gathered to be able to see. A lab attendant who came out to push the cart of urine samples into the lab noticed my stool sample, sighed, shook her head, removed it, and took it back separately into the lab.

The final medical test I required in order to obtain the certificate that would allow me to swim in the pool at Moscow State University was the blood draw. I was concerned about the safety of having blood drawn in Russia, and my fears were only heightened by a story a Russian student told me when I broached the topic with her: her parents were immigrant doctors from Africa, and knowing of the unsafe medical practices in Russia, they insisted that this child of theirs – with whom I was speaking, now a young adult, but at the time of the incident a young child -- have a new syringe used for a blood draw at school. These doctors knew a case of a child who was asked by her parents after she had her blood drawn at her school located in the same area whether a new, sterile syringe was used, and the child reported that the same syringe used on her was used on all of her classmates; an alcohol swab was used to clean the syringe before inserting it into the next child's arm. Maybe this shameful practice was due to a shortage of medical supplies at the time. When I told this student that I was scared to have my blood drawn, she assured me that now things were better and they didn't reuse syringes. I continued to impress her with my fear, and she recommended that when going in to have my blood drawn, that I inform the nurse that I had a phobia, and for this reason I should request to watch the nurse remove a new syringe to be used on me from the package. When I followed this advice and made this request of my nurse, she was clearly angry and offended. She grabbed a syringe in its package, gruffly shoved it in front of my eyes and exclaimed *Novij*! (New!), and removed it from the package. She jabbed that syringe so hard into my arm that even when thinking about it a half an hour later I thought I was going to pass out. But I got my permission slip stamped and I was allowed to use the swimming pool with the green-colored water, buried in the underground lowest level of the monstrous, 36-story, main building of Moscow State University, the Stalinist architectural monstrosity measuring over 10 million square feet in area!

Poland

On the northern coast of Poland, sitting alone on a beach on the Baltic Sea, I felt guarded, as I didn't speak Polish, and everything there was completely new to me. A little boy in the shallow water near the shore was scooping up jellyfish into his plastic toy bucket. Jellyfish were floating all around in this area of the water. As I watched the boy, he beckoned me with his hand to join him in catching jellyfish. He and I worked as a team: I would point out a jellyfish, he would catch it in his bucket, then he would take it in the bucket back to shore to show his mother, and she would act like, "Oh boy, another jellyfish." I kept expecting our silent connection to be broken by Polish words from the boy, but this never happened. We played our game for a while, and then it drew to a close. Riding on a tram away from the beach, as I reflected on the adventure of catching jellyfish in the shallow waters of the Baltic Sea, I decided then that I wanted to move to Poland. Perhaps it was due to my more regional appearance -- I am of Scandinavian descent -- that I was accepted there, or perhaps it was due to the general warm and open tolerance of the Polish people, but whatever the reason, over the course of the couple of weeks I spent in Poland on that trip, I had this sensation that I was never alone there, as if a kinship with the people followed me wherever I went. This is a sensation I have not felt in any other country I have visited. I returned to Poland soon after this trip and remained there for two years.

A language barrier didn't prevent me from having a profound experience in Poland on another occasion, when a man approached me where I was sitting beneath a prominent monument in the Old Town of Warsaw. Speaking Polish, this man opened up to me about the concern he had for his mother not being able to afford her medication; he was sobbing, really opening himself up to me. The two of us were sitting there alone. It felt to me as though the man just wanted to share his story with someone. I was afraid that he would learn that I wasn't Polish, and he would feel his trust betrayed, but my silence never became an issue, as I conveyed my sympathy silently.

I avoided speaking Polish, so as not to give myself away as a foreigner. This inhibition did not make me the best role model of a confident foreign language speaker to my English language students in Poland. How could I expect my Polish students to show confidence in speaking English with me when I was afraid of speaking their language of Polish? But I learned by working with my Polish students of those topics that were of greatest interest to them, and I focused on those topics in order to elicit more English language speech from them. A topic about which my conversational English students were inclined to speak was the Solidarity movement and the subsequent martial law imposed in order to stifle the movement (1980-81); what I learned about that period I learned from my students. During that time, vinegar was one of the only items for sale on shelves in stores throughout Poland. Surveillance cameras were installed by the communist government, the Polish United Workers' Party, on public streets throughout central Warsaw, to monitor the masses and ensure that citizens did not congregate. The law under martial law was that no more than three citizens could congregate in public. The communist government was concerned that citizens could gather in public in order to plot resistance activities against the government. The imposition of martial law caused to climax the general outrage against communism, cementing a spirit of solidarity; the political movement Solidarity was aptly named. Also, during the period of martial law in Poland in 1980-81, there was a law that forbade the direct purchase of meat from ranchers, but there was no meat for sale in the shops, so of course people broke the law and purchased meat directly from ranchers as a matter of survival. The spirit of Solidarity was characterized by an understanding that due to such unreasonable restrictions adverse to comfort, convenience, and even survival, which were imposed by the Polish United Workers' Party, citizens had to adapt their behavior in ways that otherwise would seem highly unusual and irregular. For example -- and this was a decade after the fall of the Iron Curtain -- a Pole gave me a ride home from a cafe; my apartment complex was difficult to access from the main road, as the setup of blocks of apartment buildings in relation to road access was confusing in its communist design. So, my driver, unable to find a road to my building, instead drove his car onto a twisting, paved walking path to get to my place, and a man walking his dog stepped off the sidewalk to make way for the two of us in the car. The pedestrian raised no objection, and he didn't seem to find this act of driving on the sidewalk unusual. Explaining the reaction of the pedestrian with the dog, my driver remarked, "You see? You have to do things differently under this crazy system, and everybody understands this."

There was a close-knit community of Western expats in Warsaw, the association with which made my life more pleasant, as I felt less isolated as a foreigner in Poland in their company. But limiting my socialization to the expat community also felt too insulating, so I made efforts to separate myself when possible from the expat scene; I did so in order to feel more connected to life for ordinary Poles. My Polish girlfriend helped me with daily routines like shopping and dining out, but I grew uncomfortable with her doing all of this for me. But it was a comfortable security she provided, and in its absence, I was subject to experiencing on my own situations that left me much more vulnerable and less informed. I moved to an apartment on the outskirts of Warsaw and lived there alone, to give myself a little space from the security of the expat scene and the predictable street life in the center of the city. One time in a grocery store near this new apartment, I did my shopping, and when I paid for my items, the clerk instantly alerted security. I had paid for my items using a counterfeit bill (bills are commonly examined by clerks using an infrared scanner), the possession of which and whence I had obtained it being a mystery to me.

Some months prior, in a previous apartment, my flatmate from England showed me some counterfeit bills of Polish currency he had been duped into accepting as change. It seems that foreigners are an easy target to be given counterfeit bills. I suspected that I was probably deliberately given this change in a large outdoor market in downtown Warsaw. A security guard took me into the bank of the grocery store, and I was asked where I had gotten the bill. I tried to explain myself in my limited Polish, as they kept asking me questions, trying to determine if I was involved in the production of counterfeit bills. Eventually convinced of my naiveté and that I'd been duped, I was allowed to leave. On my way out, I asked the teller what to do with the phony bill in question, and she pointed to the trash can, which is where I discarded it.

Once as I was walking alone to an internet café in Warsaw where I spent a lot of my free time socializing with my expat friends, I found myself in another situation in which the presence of a Polish acquaintance at that moment would have cleared up a misunderstanding that, as I instead had to try to make sense of it on my own, brought me great distress. Just outside of this internet café, I came upon a horrifying street scene. To me it appeared that a Neo-Nazi rally gone terribly wrong was still simmering. In the street there was a horse carcass lying on its side, rubble, and broken glass from a number of broken windows of surrounding buildings. There were some men standing along the side of the street wearing WWII Nazi uniforms. Then an advance of one line of a large number of men in WWII Nazi uniforms on horseback started moving down the street in my direction. I was terrified. I dashed into the internet café, and I sat down at a computer to log in. The café was posting updates about the events outside. I spent the next 90 minutes frantically typing to people back home, describing what was happening just outside the internet café, writing about how scared I was, explaining that I was just waiting inside the café until things settled down on the street. I went up to the bar to pay for my computer use, and I expressed concern about the events on the street to the bar maid. She smiled and shook her head, explaining that a scene for a movie was being filmed. Everything seemed so incredibly realistic - I thought that what I had witnessed was an actual, real-life event! As Warsaw took the brunt of fighting in WWII, the society at large is primed for the recreation of a scene for a movie mimicking life during the war to a ghastly degree of realism. The scene being filmed was for Roman Polanski's *The Pianist*. Now aware of what was happening, I was able to return outside to enjoy watching the brief scene being filmed.

Amsterdam, The Netherlands

The trips overseas I would take in my twenties were usually short trips on a limited budget, for which I would make no advanced arrangements. Upon landing on a Sunday morning at Schiphol Airport, Amsterdam, I needed to exchange currency as a first priority, but I could not find any currency exchange offices that were open in the limited area of the airport where I searched, so I decided to walk all the way into the city of Amsterdam in order to try to find a currency exchange office. Could I not have assumed before starting out that because it was a Sunday, there almost certainly would not be any currency exchange offices open in the city of Amsterdam either? Yes, but my feet were driving me to explore against my better sense. In the open air near the airport, I trotted across two roads running in opposite directions of a busy, multi-lane freeway. I was not exactly sure how to get to Amsterdam from there. Just on the other side of the freeway I had crossed, there was a path designated for non-motorized traffic running alongside a field. I encountered a young man on a bicycle there, and I asked him, "Which way to Amsterdam?" The man waved his arm in the general direction of Amsterdam, and I headed in the direction he indicated, across fields, over a stream, through a wooded area -- all areas free of people -- until eventually I reached the outskirts of Amsterdam. I kept walking into and through Amsterdam, until, after walking roughly eleven miles from the airport, the road I was on came to an end in front of the main railway station in central Amsterdam. And who should I encounter there, in front of the railway station? The same man on the bicycle who had given me directions to Amsterdam outside the airport, nearly 11 miles back. Seeing me, he remarked, "I see you found Amsterdam."

There were no currency exchange offices, either open or closed, to be found in the small area of my search in the center of Amsterdam. I wasn't disappointed though, for the interesting scenery new and foreign to me was ample reward for my effort. I likely didn't even bother to ask anyone where a currency exchange office could be found there in the center of Amsterdam. I just turned around and walked all the way back to the airport, because my travel-happy feet were dominating many brain functions. My journey by foot from Schiphol Airport to the center of Amsterdam and back took eleven hours. I successfully relied on my strong sense of direction to find my way back to the airport. Returning to the airport, I was exhausted. It was approaching 11 p.m. I rolled out my sleeping bag to sleep that night on the airport floor, but two airport security officers approached to inform me that I couldn't sleep on the airport floor. I shared the story with the two security officers of my adventurous journey by foot from the airport to the city center and back. I hoped that they would have sympathy for me in my exhausted state, and that they would allow me to sleep on the floor of the airport. In fact, the two security officers did agree to allow me to spend the night sleeping on the airport floor in my sleeping bag. They promised to awaken me early the next morning before the airport got busy. I was up and gone before the time when the security guards were to rouse me.

I started walking that morning from the airport along the shoulder of the same freeway I had crossed at a sprint the day before. I was once again going into Amsterdam. I was spared another long and strenuous trip by foot into Amsterdam this time, as an airport shuttle filled with passengers heading into Amsterdam pulled to the side of the freeway, just in front of where I was walking, to welcome me aboard. I wasn't even near a bus stop -- the driver just made a special stop in order to give me a ride into the city. Once I arrived in Amsterdam, getting new shoes was my first priority: my feet were blistered and in pain from walking so much the day before; the shoes I had been wearing were not suitable for walking long distances. I found a shoe shore where I bought a nice pair of blue, Dutch sneakers. All the walking from the prior day had put me in a good frame of mind to appreciate some quiet rush hour traffic comprised exclusively of bicycles, which passed through the area where I was sitting (near the shoe store). Next, I went in search of food, as I was very hungry, having burned so many calories from walking so much the day before. I found a bakery advertised as the oldest bakery in Amsterdam, and there I bought a delicious, dense loaf of sugar bread. I went outside, and seated in front of the bakery's front window, I devoured the entire loaf of sugar bread for all the bakery customers and employees to see. I must have been an amusing sight for them, with my unusually hearty appetite.

Romania

1998 was the year I traveled to Romania. At that time, U.S. citizens were permitted to travel for up to 90 days in Romania with only a U.S. passport; no tourist visa was required. Such visa-free travel for up to three months in Romania was not a right enjoyed by citizens of most nations, and in fact, a number of the Romanian authorities who checked my passport were unaware of the visa exception for Americans. The problem with this arose for the first time at customs in the Bucharest airport: I was asked by the agent examining my passport where my visa was. I explained to her that as a U.S. citizen, I had the right to travel in Romania for up to 90 days with a passport but without a visa, so hearing this, the agent stamped my passport, but she acted a little hesitant about doing so. Clearing customs inside the airport and a mob of aggressive taxi drivers soliciting passengers outside the airport, I boarded a public bus bound for Bucharest.

In some randomly chosen bustling area of Bucharest, I got off the bus and walked a short distance to a nearby park. In the park on a bench sat a young woman a few years younger than me. She was seated at one end of the bench. I sat down on the other end of the bench and, as I began a conversation with her in English, she slid closer to me. She enjoyed the opportunity to speak English with a native speaker. We talked, as dusk descended. The bats began to fly between the trees. My park bench companion, whose name was Dorota, asked me where I was staying, and I told her that I had no lodging for the night. She suggested that I wait with her until her male friend returned to his dormitory, which was located a short distance from where we were sitting, and she would ask him if I could spend the night in his dorm room. At around 10:30 p.m., Dorota's friend returned to the dormitory, and she discussed my situation with him. I could tell from her friend's body language when they were speaking that he was not in favor of the idea of allowing me to spend the night in his dorm room. Dorota came back and apologized that I couldn't stay with her friend, but she offered to meet me back in the park the next day, so that she could give me a tour of Bucharest. I should have asked Dorota to help me get a room in a hotel, but my preference at this time of my life was to travel without accommodations; I felt that staying in a hotel room would deprive me of an opportunity to get a less filtered feel for the country.

Dorota and I agreed to meet in the park the next morning. (Unfortunately, I could not find the park the next day, so I never saw Dorota again.) Meanwhile, I was off to who knows where, into the night, into the city of Bucharest, a city completely unfamiliar to me, where I knew not what to expect. The first thing I saw right near me as I exited the park was a woman using a knife to fend off two men who were harassing her. Central Bucharest is a no-sit-down-area, where enormous sections of concrete cover large areas – a soul-draining, communist concrete expanse in a dead zone for architectural aesthetics. I was looking for a place to sit down so that I could get my bearings by studying my map of Bucharest, but there were absolutely no benches anywhere in sight. If I got away from the main square, I thought, I'd find a place to sit down. I found a place to sit down in a dark alley off the main square, and there I tried to make out what I could on my map, so that I could at least get some sense of the area. I then returned in the direction of the better-lighted main square of flat concrete expanse. Before I could make my way there, I was suddenly surrounded by a pack of seven or eight aggressive street dogs. Fortunately for me, I was carrying a Swiss Army knife in my pocket. I opened the largest blade and used it effectively to fend off the dogs without my being bitten, spinning around in turn to fend off whichever of the dogs attempted to lunge at me from one moment to the next. I escaped the circle of dogs without any of them or me being harmed, and leaving this panic situation, I passed a police officer who was sitting in his patrol car; he had witnessed the incident, and he asked me in English with a strong foreign accent, "Is there a problem?" He asked in a way that conveyed little interest in helping me.

Just when I made my way back to the main square, after having nearly been torn to bits by a pack of aggressive street dogs, I was approached by two young men in police uniforms. They asked to see my passport, and when they discovered that I didn't have a visa, I was once again put on the defensive to explain that U.S. citizens were not required to have a visa for travel in Romania for up to 90 days. These men were not interested in accepting my legally valid defense. I was told "Internment" would be stamped on my passport, I would spend the night in jail, then I would be required to take a return flight to the U.S., and I would not be allowed to return to Romania for five years. The two men showed me a section in a flip book of laws printed in the Romanian language, which I couldn't read, to support the legal course for me that they had outlined. Again, I defended my legal right as a U.S. citizen to travel in Romania for up to 90 days without a visa. I tried to appeal to their good side in any way possible, acknowledging to their question that, indeed, I was drawn to Romania due to a fascination with the legend of Dracula, and finally, after my protracted effort to try to convince them to act leniently, they decided that they would let me off with a fine.

The fine that I paid in cash to the two men in uniform was an amount sufficient to buy eight to ten round-trip tickets by train to neighboring cities, or to buy the same number of Romanian-made tennis shoes. Once I paid the fine, the men acted as though they were there to help me, recommending a hotel in which I could stay and a taxi company to use in order to get to that hotel; there were disreputable taxi companies in the city, the men cautioned me, and I must be careful not to be cheated. The taxi I rode in pulled up to the recommended hotel, but to my bewilderment I saw that the hotel was a vacant, unfinished, concrete shell of a building without any windows installed. But fortunately, this unfinished hotel was located right next to the train station, and that was the place I wanted to be. My stress level was elevated after these encounters, first with the pack of aggressive street dogs, and then with the two men in uniform, and I felt it imperative to get into the safety of the train station. A heavy, padlocked chain wrapped around the bars of two glass doors into the train station prevented my entry, but I shook and shook the bars of the doors until someone came to unlock the padlocked chain to let me inside. Once inside, I was directed into a seating room full of other passengers who were waiting overnight for their morning departures. A man in uniform entered the room abruptly to check everyone's passports. My stomach sank, anticipating another "Where's your visa?" question -- and that's exactly what I got when this man in uniform looked at my passport. Again, I explained my right as a U.S. citizen to travel for up to 90 days in Romania without a visa. The man in uniform handed my passport back to me, then informed me, "I'll deal with you later." I was petrified. I didn't flinch a muscle in my seat as I sat there until daybreak. Two Romanian middle-aged men seated near me seemed amused by my petrified state, but they sat slumped with their heads lowered. This man in uniform never did return to deal with me.

Later that morning in the train station, I was talking to a young Romania man, likely a college student, about my problems with getting fined by the men in police uniforms the night before. This new acquaintance with whom I was conversing explained to me that it was a common scam in Bucharest for young men to dress up in uniforms, pretending to be police officers. One should never give these fake policemen money, this new acquaintance explained to me, no matter how much they insisted. I felt a little relieved to learn that what had happened to me was a scam. A naïve foreigner would not consider challenging such convincing, fake authority in this situation, and the scammers know this.

By the time I arrived by train in Brasov, Transylvania, from Bucharest, I had decided to hitchhike, so that I could get a better feel for the country than I could from a train window. I walked to the outskirts of Brasov, then I asked some teenage boys I encountered how a person hitchhikes in Romania. There was a small group of people gathered along the roadside also looking for rides, and I was put in front on the first stopped vehicle as a way of honoring the foreign guest in their country. My ride was in a lorry: a male driver and his male friend. We were soon heading down a country road. After a while the driver pulled over to give a ride to a hefty peasant woman dressed in a head scarf and a floral-print dress who was also hitching for a ride, and we all bounced down the road through rural Transylvania, squeezed together in the lorry cab.

My driver dropped me off at the train station in Cluj-Napoca, Romania, at about 10:45 p.m. I was making good progress hitchhiking, so I decided to continue traveling in this manner, rather than take a train. A short time later, walking in the dark, I passed a tavern, where a man in uniform appeared from the darkness in front of me and asked to see my passport, and then – No surprise! – he wanted to know where my visa was. Somehow, I explained my way out of this situation, and I continued on, keyed up. Away from the outside lights of the tavern and back into the darkness, a car passed me, went up the road a short distance, and then its lights cut out. From the direction of this car through the pitch darkness suddenly appeared a man, presumably the driver of the car, the lights of which had been cut out. I was so alarmed by the man's sudden appearance that I let out a horrific mouthful of gibberish that seemed to startle the stranger approaching enough to protect me from his further advance. I walked on and on in the pitch dark on a desolate country road in rural Transylvania. My biggest fear there was of being attacked by a wild animal. Eventually, near the Romania-Hungary border on the Romanian side, I passed through a quiet village, and my alien presence late at night aroused the barking of what seemed to be hundreds of dogs, surely waking everyone in the small village, as I made my not-so-stealthy advance toward the border. The final area I had to pass through out of Romania came in the form of what felt like an informal, civilian border checkpoint: a young man was standing behind his car with the hatchback open, listening to music with his friends, and he kept asking me a lot of peculiar questions, as if screening me to consider if I should be permitted to continue toward the border. I passed his screening and walked onward, toward, and then through the border into Hungary.

Hungary

My hitchhiking experience in Hungary was much less successful than my hitchhiking experience in Romania. Walking on and on without being offered a ride, I estimated, based on road signs, that I walked 35 miles in one day. Before this, I did get two rides, and these were rather intense experiences. A businessman gave me a ride, and despite the air of normalcy and calm he projected (this air strengthened by his nice car and professional appearance), he drove dangerously and at great speed. I had to look out the side window for most of the ride; I felt safer not seeing what his automobile was approaching with insane rapidity, such as the much slower traffic that included horse-drawn carts. One time when my driver depressed firmly on the brake, I counted to the number eight to myself as he continued to brake, and even after that he was still driving way too fast. The next driver to give me a ride as I hitchhiked through Hungary was a double-trailer lorry operator. This driver also made daring traffic moves, but he was an excellent, exciting driver, not reckless like the businessman before. I felt through the language barrier that my job was to be a second pair of eyes on the night road for this lorry driver. The roads twisted around like spaghetti noodles and they started to look the same, so much so that I nearly accused the driver of backtracking – not that he would understand my accusation anyway, due to the language barrier. Notably, both Hungarian drivers, when they stopped their vehicles to go into some establishments, left me alone in their vehicles with the keys in the ignitions. Maybe I seemed trustworthy, even though I didn't speak their language.

One night in Budapest, I rolled out my sleeping bag on a bench in a children's park in order to sleep there for the night. I awoke late at night in heavy fog to the sound of a human voice shouting "Rooooohhh!" very loudly somewhere nearby. I was terrified, shaking, and I frantically rolled up my sleeping bag and left the park.

Walking along the road near Gyor, Hungary, a shuttle bus pulled over to give me a ride. I wasn't even signaling for a ride, it just pulled over. I got in and headed to the back of the bus, understanding from the driver's body language that the ride wouldn't cost me anything. There were other youths aboard; the bus was bound for the nearest youth hostel in Gyor, where it would drop off its passengers. Shortly after I boarded the bus, a mysterious sand storm formed. A couple more teenagers were collected out of the sand storm and we made our way to the hostel. I showered for the first time in many days, but I opted not to take a room, as I wanted to travel without accommodations, so I continued by foot down the road.

The dot on the map representing Szombathely, Hungary placed the town right next to the border with Austria, so, as the distance on the map didn't seem far, my plan was to cross into Austria by foot from Szombathely (this last point of my journey through Hungary to Szombathely I arrived at by train). In Szombathely, while trying to make my way to the border, five or six men in their twenties were coming down the sidewalk toward me, and I felt as though they intended to assault me, or that they might try to rob me, so in a panic of self-defense, I verbalized to them the few Hungarian words I had learned while hitchhiking in the country. Then I asked the group of young men for a cigarette and a light, and the fact that I tried to use some words in their language, combined with the common bond I held with them of smoking, reversed their attitude to one of camaraderie with me. Suddenly, they were there to assist me. When I explained that I was heading to the border, they suggested that I take a taxi cab, and one of them called for a taxi for me from a nearby pay phone, but no taxi would take me to the border, for obvious reasons. Knowing I would have to walk, they pointed down a main road that led to the border. It was approaching 11 p.m. by this time; as I watched a vehicle pass by, down the road on which I was headed, I would see how the red tail lights of the vehicle would move up and down over a couple of hills, not braking for the border (which I expected to be quite close), until eventually the tail lights were out of sight. I kept walking and walking, and then finally, I came upon a large, green road sign that indicated that the border lay three kilometers ahead. This area was unpopulated countryside, and it was completely dark. Suddenly I was blinded by a bright light shone directly into my face. I was completely ambushed, and one of two men standing before me was yelling at me to show him my passport, which fortunately I had in a chest pocket, within easy reach. It was the Hungarian Border Patrol, and the agent was yelling at me in a language I couldn't understand, presumably Hungarian, and all I could say in response was, "Ich verstehe nicht." The border patrol agent started parroting me in a loud, mocking voice: "Ich verstehe nicht! Ich verstehe nicht!" They thought they had caught someone trying to sneak across the border into Austria (pre-EU), presumably from a poorer country. So, when the agents looked at my passport and learned that I was an American, they changed their attitude toward me completely. One of the border agents gave me a sandwich and poured me some tea from his thermos, and then they gave me a ride in their patrol car the remaining distance to the border! As we made our way in the car to the border, one of the agents, rather stunned, informed me that in the five years he had been working that job, I was the first American he had "caught" trying to cross the border; his use of the word "caught" was meant facetiously, as Americans were guests regarded favorably in that part of the world.

Austria

I was allowed to cross the border into Austria with minimal screening. The supervisor of the agent who allowed me through though, felt that his subordinate agent hadn't screened me carefully enough, so the supervisor instructed his subordinate to inspect my rucksack. The supervisor then observed as the subordinate agent gave my rucksack a cursory inspection. It was dark and late by this time, and I headed out into the darkness uphill on a pitch-black road, into the Austrian countryside. In my state of exhaustion brought on by having walked so many miles through Hungary, I half-imagined that a large bird swooped down and brushed past me as I walked uphill. I felt I was in no shape to continue, so I returned down the hill to the Austrian border checkpoint. If this stretch of road had offered a place where it seemed safe to do so, I would have slept beside the road, instead of returning to the border station for help. Back at the Austrian border station, I explained to the same supervisor who had seen me through that I was completely exhausted, and that I was afraid that if I kept walking on into the night down that road, that I would die. The supervisor offered sympathy in a quiet and professional manner, and he bought me a cup of hot chocolate from the vending machine. Since I obviously couldn't rest at the border station, he suggested that I ask one of the lorry drivers coming in from Hungary for a ride to the nearest town in Austria, but he made it clear that I should ask in German for a ride from the driver. By the time a lorry pulled up, I had my request for a ride in German worked out in my head. The driver obliged, and I got in. But I was so exhausted that I couldn't stay awake in the lorry for the short distance to the nearest town, and I would only realize that I had fallen asleep when I would feel the lorry driver push me back to my side of the cab after I had slumped over to sleep toward him – at least I believe that was what was happening. With a start I was awakened when reaching the nearest town in Austria just across the border, and now outside the lorry, I stumbled in a half-awake state into a very brightly-lit gas station. I wandered in and looked around, but I didn't buy anything, since I didn't have any Austrian schillings. I walked away from the gas station, crossed a quiet, narrow road a short distance away, and stepped over a mound of dirt to the sunken foundation of a building construction site, out of view from the road and private. I rolled out my sleeping bag and slept at the construction site until morning.

When I awoke and opened my eyes that morning, I saw a bright, clear, blue sky overhead, and I heard the birds chirping. Back beside the road, I expected another unsuccessful day of hitchhiking, such as I had experienced in Hungary. But the first vehicle to approach on that quiet road pulled over for me. My new, young, male driver was headed to a flea market in Vienna to sell the few pieces of furniture he had in his car. I rode with him to Vienna, sleeping the entire two hours in his back seat. Thank you, kind driver, whose name I never got!

On this trip, I had ample funds to travel more comfortably, but I had planned for a trip of some duration (which I cut short), so I was trying to economize for a long trip. Besides, traveling without accommodations brought greater adventure. I looked on my map of Vienna for green spaces – parks -- where I could sleep. I made my way to one of the parks on the map, where I discovered a perfect space for sleeping: a large bush at its base had a deep, hollowed-out shape, a perfect cocoon fit of an exact length, width, and height for my body to fit in, and in my green, military, mummy-style sleeping bag, I was well concealed. I slept there for two nights; it was a great experience for me to sleep tucked away in a bush in a public park in the magnificent city of Vienna, and waking at a construction site as my first taste of Austria was thrilling.

Morocco

I crossed the Sea of Gibraltar by ferry from Spain into Tangiers, Morrocco. Once in Tangiers, I needed to exchange currency, but it was a Sunday, and there were no currency exchange offices open. A young man named Omar approached me, and he asked me if I needed any help. I told him I needed to exchange currency, so Omar asked several people at an outdoor café if any of them would exchange U.S. dollars for Moroccan dirhams; eventually Omar found someone who would exchange. Next, Omar took me to an outdoor market to buy a traditional, full-length, men's Moroccan gown, a type that I had told him I was interested in buying. Wow, what a friendly and helpful guy! ... Or so it seemed. Omar then suggested that we go to an outdoor café for some coffee. Wow, what a great friend I had found! (I didn't really feel this way.) When we finished our coffee, I could tell that Omar expected me to pay for it. Well, it's the least I could do, since he helped me to exchange currency and to find a Moroccan men's gown for purchase.

How else could this attentive man help me? I needed lodging, and Omar helped me find that: $7 a night for a room? I must be in paradise! I paid for my hotel room, then I bid Omar farewell outside the hotel; he stood there like a bellhop expecting his tip. I gave Omar a modest but fair gratuity, and he was on his way, perhaps acting a bit slighted.

In my room on an upper level of the hotel, I was spooked by the sound of two white Westerners beating on hand drums in a hypnotic fashion somewhere nearby in the open-air space between rooms. A quick check on all fours in a culture shock panic in my room revealed no snakes or their holes of entry in the concrete floor and lower walls under the bed. This panic attack subsided after I scrawled a feverish letter to someone back home; I was then calmed down enough to rest for the night. In the morning, I headed out in search of food and drink. Near a corner store, two beggars, intent on getting money from me, started to follow me; I firmly, repeatedly told them "No" to their importuning. I then walked into the corner store, partly to get away from the men, but they kept pestering me for money as I tried to shop. Outside the shop, the men kept following me, asking for money. I threatened that I would get the police involved, and one of the crooks replied, "You want to go to the police? Go to the police. We saw you smoking hashish with Omar yesterday. [Untrue] We can make problems for you."

So, Omar was involved with these petty criminals, and I was targeted and set up on my first day in Tangiers. I was wearing the full-length gown Omar had helped me to buy the preceding day, and underneath the gown, in my money belt, my substantial stash of cash was well-protected from the extortionists. Naively, I felt safer possessing all of my money in cash for the trip on my person than I did relying on an ATM bank card. I reached into the front pockets of my gown and gave them all the money I had there, the equivalent of thirty-five U.S. dollars in Moroccan dirhams.

One of the two crooks demanded the silver ring I was wearing, which I had bought in Jerusalem. I was sick about having to part with that beautiful ring! One of the crooks seemed to be more sympathetic, and he tried to help convince the other surlier one that I had given them enough by that point. The surlier of the two finally acquiesced, and fortunately, they never got to my cache of money; my magic gown kept my money safe – exactly as I had planned! But I decided to leave Morocco after this terrible experience, so I immediately took a ferry back to Spain.

Spain

On a train in southern Spain, in the cabin to which I was assigned, there was a child with his arms and legs propped straight out to his sides in casts and braces. His mother sat beside him. There were two or three other passengers in the same cabin. The crippled child took up the thought in the room. I began to compose a poem. Words on paper and tears down my face started flowing. This poem, which I entitled "Train Ride Requiem," just came out, line after line, in that train cabin. My sobbing in the small space was as obvious as the child's crippled condition. I tried to conceal from the other passengers in the small compartment my tears by putting a shirt over my face, but the space was too confined. It flowed: lines of poetry, tears from my eyes.

Israel

In April of 1997, I traveled to Israel, bringing with me a mountain bike, intent on riding it to Mt. Sinai, Egypt from Tel Aviv after my arrival at Ben Gurion Airport. I guess I didn't have a firm idea of the distance – probably relying beforehand on my "it doesn't look that far on the map" navigation; in actuality, the distance is 332 miles. I'm not sure how I thought I could budget that bicycle trip either, as I flew over to Israel with only $350 in my possession. I was naïve, expecting Israel to be as cheap as some of the countries I had visited in Central and Eastern Europe (though this small sum of money wouldn't have gone far in those places either). As I entered Ben Gurion Airport and collected my bicycle, an airport employee asked me what I planned to do with my bicycle, and I informed her that I planned to ride it to Mt. Sinai, Egypt, whereupon she told me that she thought that would be "very, very, very, very, very, very, very, very dangerous." Direct quote: she used the word "very" eight times; I figured eight "very"s was enough to make me rethink my plan. I decided instead to take a taxi to Jerusalem, so I locked my bicycle up to a metal railing in front of Ben Gurion Airport; my bicycle was waiting for me when I returned to the airport 24 hours later, which in itself is peculiar: against the backdrop of the intense security exercised at that airport, there stood a lone bicycle locked to a metal rail in front of the airport.

I spent most of my $350 quite quickly in the City of David, Jerusalem. I bought interesting gifts for my family, and after that, I could barely afford to be there for the rest of the day, let alone the month for which I had made my flight itinerary. While shopping in the City of David, I asked one shopkeeper who was wearing a white gown and a red keffiyeh if he had any rings for sale, and he told me, "I will show you the Rings of Death." I took that as my cue to leave his shop.

So, almost out of money in a tense country, I changed my return flight date at a cost of $25 (this was the rate to change a flight date offered by the youth travel agency from which I bought my ticket; this option always gave me a feeling of flexibility to leave a place sooner if I wanted). I then called the cab driver who had given me his business card when he transported me from Tel Aviv to Jerusalem. I placed my call to the cab driver from a pay phone on a noisy, congested street; I could only provide the driver with sketchy details as to my location, but by some marvel, the cab driver found me and took me to the airport in Tel Aviv.

The security at Ben Gurion Airport, as I experienced it, was impressive and a little intimidating. First there's the interview at a table where the traveler stands in front of his luggage placed on a table, as an inspector looks through the luggage and asks the traveler questions; this is before the traveler goes to the check-in desk. But the fact that I had originally booked a flight itinerary for one month, but abruptly changed it for immediate return after less than a day in the country, aroused suspicion. Security personnel took me back into a room and I had to strip to my underwear in a partitioned small area behind a curtain while they looked through every item of my luggage, even opening the small film canisters I had in my baggage. But not finding any contraband, they released me. So much time had passed during my interview and secondary screening that I missed my flight. But I was booked on another flight, and I was escorted to my gate by a courteous, young male staff member who walked so rapidly, as was necessary in order to cover the great distance in the airport in time to make it to the gate from which my flight would soon be departing, that it was difficult for me to keep pace with him.

How I got here to this tiny scratch of nothingness is beyond me. If my friends could see me now, they'd have great eyesight. Travelling now, I'm using low-grade road English. Effortlessly I breeze across stiff continents.

On a long travel,

You get to where you're going,

And along the way,

Total strangers

Seem to be expecting you.